PENGUIN CLASSICS

SERIES ADVISOR: PHILIP HORNE

DAISY MILLER

HENRY JAMES was born in 1843 in Washington Place, New York, of Scottish and Irish ancestry. His father was a prominent theologian and philosopher and his elder brother, William, also became famous as a philosopher. James attended schools in New York and later in London, Paris and Geneva, before briefly entering the Law School at Harvard in 1862. In 1865 he began to contribute reviews and short stories to American journals. He visited Europe twice as an adult before moving to Paris in 1875, where he met Flaubert, Turgenev and other literary figures. However, after a year he moved to London, where he met with such success in society that he confessed to accepting 107 invitations in the winter of 1878–9 alone. In 1898 he left London and went to live at Lamb House, Rye, Sussex. Henry James became a naturalized British citizen in 1915, and was awarded the Order of Merit in 1916, shortly before his death in February of that year.

In addition to many short stories, plays, books of criticism, biography and autobiography, and much travel writing, he wrote some twenty novels, the first of which, *Watch and Ward*, appeared serially in the *Atlantic Monthly* in 1870. His novella 'Daisy Miller' (1878) established him as a literary figure on both sides of the Atlantic. Other novels include *Roderick Hudson* (1875), *The American* (1877), *The Europeans* (1878), *Washington Square* (1880), *The Portrait of a Lady* (1881), *The Bostonians* (1886), *The Princess Casamassima* (1886), *The Tragic Muse* (1890), *The Spoils of Poynton* (1897), *What Maisie Knew* (1897), *The Awkward Age* (1899), *The Wings of the Dove* (1902), *The Ambassadors* (1903) and *The Golden Bowl* (1904).

DAVID LODGE was born in London in 1935. He taught in the English Department of the University of Birmingham from 1960 until 1987, when he retired to become a full-time writer. He is Emeritus Professor of English Literature at Birmingham and lives in that city. He is a Fellow of the Royal Society of Literature, was awarded a CBE for services to literature and is also a Chevalier de l'Ordre des Arts et des Lettres. He is the author of many novels and numerous works of literary criticism, the most recent of which are *Author, Author* (2004) and *The Year of Henry James* (2006).

PHILIP HORNE is a Professor of English at University College London. He is the author of *Henry James and Revision: The New York Edition* (1990); editor of *Henry James: A Life in Letters* (1999); and co-editor of *Thorold Dickinson; A World of Film* (2008). He has also edited Henry James, *A London Life & The Reverberator*; and for Penguin, Henry James, *The Tragic Muse*, and Charles Dickens, *Oliver Twist*. He has written articles on Henry James, and on a wide range of other subjects, including telephones and literature, zombies and consumer culture, the films of Powell and Pressburger and Martin Scorsese, the texts of Emily Dickinson, and the criticism of F. R. Leavis.

HENRY JAMES

Daisy Miller

A Study

Edited with an Introduction and Notes by
DAVID LODGE

PENGUIN BOOKS

PENGUIN BOOKS

An imprint of Penguin Random House LLC
375 Hudson Street
New York, New York 10014
penguin.com

First published 1878
Published with an introduction in Penguin Books 2007

ISBN 978-0-14-144134-4

Printed in the United States of America

ScoutAutomatedPrintCode

Contents

Contents

Chronology

1843 *15 April*: HJ born at 21 Washington Place in New York City, second of five children of Henry James (1811–82), speculative theologian and social thinker, whose strict entrepreneur father had amassed wealth estimated at $3 million, one of the top ten American fortunes of his time, and his wife Mary (1810–82), daughter of James Walsh, a New York cotton merchant of Scottish family.

1843–5 Accompanies parents to Paris and London.

1845–7 James family returns to USA and settles in Albany, NY.

1847–55 Family settles in New York City; HJ taught by tutors and in private schools.

1855–8 Family travels in Europe: Geneva, London, Paris, Boulogne-sur-Mer. Returns to USA and settles in Newport, Rhode Island.

1859–60 Family in Europe again: HJ attends scientific school, then the Academy (later the University) in Geneva. Learns German in Bonn.

September 1860: Family returns to Newport. HJ makes friends with future critic T. S. Perry (who records that HJ 'was continually writing stories, mainly of a romantic kind') and artist John La Farge.

1861–3 Injures his back helping to extinguish a fire in Newport and is exempted from military service in American Civil War (1861–5).

Autumn 1862: Enters Harvard Law School for a term. Begins to send stories to magazines.

1864 *February*: First short story, 'A Tragedy of Error', published anonymously in *Continental Monthly*.

May: Family moves to 13 Ashburton Place, Boston, Massachusetts.

October: Unsigned review published in *North American Review*.

1865 *March*: First signed tale, 'The Story of a Year', appears in *Atlantic Monthly*. HJ's criticism published in first number of the *Nation* (New York).

1866–8 Continues reviewing and writing stories.

Summer 1866: W. D. Howells, novelist, critic and influential editor, becomes a friend.

November: Family moves to 20 Quincy Street, beside Harvard Yard, in Cambridge, Massachusetts.

1869 Travels for his health to England, where he meets John Ruskin, William Morris, Charles Darwin and George Eliot; also visits Switzerland and Italy.

1870 *March*: Death in America of his much-loved cousin Minny Temple.

May: HJ, still unwell, is reluctantly back in Cambridge.

1871 *August–December*: First short novel, *Watch and Ward*, serialized in *Atlantic Monthly*.

1872–4 Accompanies invalid sister Alice and aunt Catherine Walsh ('Aunt Kate') to Europe in May. Writes travel pieces for the *Nation*. Between October 1872 and September 1874 spends periods of time in Paris, Rome, Switzerland, Homburg and Italy without his family.

Spring 1874: Begins first long novel, *Roderick Hudson*, in Florence.

September: Returns to USA.

1875 *January*: Publishes *A Passionate Pilgrim, and Other Tales*, his first work to appear in book form. It is followed by *Transatlantic Sketches* (travel pieces) and then by *Roderick Hudson* (November). Spends six months in New York City (111 East 25th Street), then three in Cambridge.

11 November: Arrives at 29 rue de Luxembourg, Paris as correspondent for the *New York Tribune*.

December: Begins new novel, *The American*.

1876 Meets Gustave Flaubert, Ivan Turgenev, Edmond de Goncourt, Alphonse Daudet, Guy de Maupassant and Emile Zola.

December: Moves to London and settles at 3 Bolton Street, just off Piccadilly.

1877 Visits Paris, Florence and Rome.

May: *The American* is published.

1878 Meets William Gladstone, Alfred Tennyson, and Robert Browning.

February: Collection of essays, *French Poets and Novelists*, is the first book HJ publishes in London.

July: Novella 'Daisy Miller' serialized in *The Cornhill Magazine*; in November Harper's publish it in the USA, establishing HJ's reputation on both sides of the Atlantic.

September: Publishes *The Europeans* (novel).

1879 *December*: Publishes *Confidence* (novel) and *Hawthorne* (critical study).

1880 *December*: Publishes *Washington Square* (novel).

1881 *October*: Returns to USA; visits Cambridge, Mass.

November: Publishes *The Portrait of a Lady* (novel).

1882 *January*: Death of mother. Visits New York and Washington, D.C.

May: Travels back to England but returns to USA on death of father in December.

1883 *Summer*: Returns to London.

November: Fourteen-volume collected edition of fiction published by Macmillan.

December: Publishes *Portraits of Places* (travel writings).

1884 Sister Alice moves to London and settles near HJ.

September: Publishes *A Little Tour in France* (travel writings) and *Tales of Three Cities*; his important artistic statement 'The Art of Fiction' appears in *Longman's Magazine*.

Becomes a friend of R. L. Stevenson and Edmund Gosse. Writes to his American friend Grace Norton: 'I shall never marry . . . I am both happy enough and miserable enough, as it is.'

1885–6 Publishes two serial novels, *The Bostonians* and *The Princess Casamassima*.

6 March 1886: Moves into flat at 34 de Vere Gardens.

1887 *Spring and summer:* Visits Florence and Venice. Continues friendship (begun in 1880) with American novelist Constance Fenimore Woolson.

1888 Publishes *The Reverberator* (novel), 'The Aspern Papers' (novella) and *Partial Portraits* (criticism).

1889 Collection of tales, *A London Life*, published.

1890 *The Tragic Muse* (novel) published.

1891 Play version of *The American* has a short run in the provinces and London.

1892 *February:* Publishes *The Lesson of the Master* (story collection).

March: Death of Alice James in London.

1893 Three volumes of tales published: *The Real Thing* (March), *The Private Life* (June), *The Wheel of Time* (September).

1894 Deaths of Constance Fenimore Woolson and R. L. Stevenson.

1895 *5 January:* Play *Guy Domville* is greeted by boos and applause on its première at St James's Theatre; HJ abandons playwriting for many years.

Visits Ireland. Takes up cycling. Publishes two volumes of tales, *Terminations* (May) and *Embarrassments* (June).

1896 Publishes *The Other House* (novel).

1897 Two novels, *The Spoils of Poynton* and *What Maisie Knew*, published.

February: Starts dictating, due to wrist problems.

September: Takes lease on Lamb House, Rye, Sussex.

1898 *June:* Moves into Lamb House. Sussex neighbours include the writers Joseph Conrad, H. G. Wells and Ford Madox Hueffer (Ford).

August: Publishes *In the Cage* (short novel).

October: 'The Turn of the Screw', ghost story included in *The Two Magics*, proves his most popular work since 'Daisy Miller'.

1899 *April:* Novel *The Awkward Age* published.

August: Buys the freehold of Lamb House.

1900 Shaves off his beard.

August: Publishes collection of tales, *The Soft Side*.

Friendship with American novelist Edith Wharton develops.

1901 *February*: Publishes novel *The Sacred Fount*.

1902 *August*: Publishes novel *The Wings of the Dove*.

1903 *February*: Publishes collection of tales *The Better Sort*.

September: Publishes novel *The Ambassadors*.

October: Publishes memoir *William Wetmore Story and his Friends*.

1904 *August*: Sails to USA, his first visit for twenty-one years. Travels to New England, New York, Philadelphia, Washington, the South, St Louis, Chicago, Los Angeles and San Francisco.

November: Publishes novel *The Golden Bowl*.

1905 *January*: Is President Theodore Roosevelt's guest at the White House. Elected to the American Academy of Arts and Letters.

July: Back in Lamb House, begins revising works for the New York Edition of *The Novels and Tales of Henry James*.

October: Publishes *English Hours* (travel essays).

1906–8 Selects, arranges, prefaces and has illustrations made for New York Edition (published 1907–9, twenty-four volumes).

1907 *January*: Publishes *The American Scene* (travel essays).

1908 *March*: Play *The High Bid* produced at Edinburgh.

1909 *October*: Publishes *Italian Hours* (travel essays).

Health problems.

1910 *August*: Travels to USA with brother William, who dies a week after their return.

October: Publishes *The Finer Grain* (tales).

1911 *August*: Returns to England.

October: Publishes *The Outcry* (novel adapted from play).

Begins work on autobiography.

1912 *June*: Receives honorary doctorate from Oxford University.

October: Takes flat at 21 Carlyle Mansions, Cheyne Walk, Chelsea; suffers from shingles.

1913 *March*: Publishes *A Small Boy and Others* (first volume of autobiography).

Portrait painted by John Singer Sargent for seventieth birthday (15 April).

1914 *March*: Publishes *Notes of a Son and Brother* (second volume of autobiography).

August: Outbreak of World War One; HJ becomes passionately engaged with the British cause and helps Belgian refugees and wounded soldiers.

October: Publishes *Notes on Novelists*.

1915 Is made honorary president of the American Volunteer Motor Ambulance Corps.

July: Becomes a British citizen.

Writes essays about the war (collected in *Within the Rim*, 1919) and the Preface to *Letters from America* (1916) by the poet Rupert Brooke, who died the previous year.

2 December: Suffers a stroke.

1916 Awarded the Order of Merit in New Year Honours.

28 February: Dies. After his funeral in Chelsea Old Church, his ashes are smuggled back to America by sister-in-law and buried in the family plot in Cambridge, Massachusetts.

Philip Horne

Introduction

First-time readers of 'Daisy Miller' should be aware that details of the plot are revealed in the course of this introduction.

THE PLACE OF 'DAISY MILLER' IN JAMES'S LIFE AND WORK

'Daisy Miller', first published as a magazine serial in the summer of 1878, has a very special place in the history of Henry James's literary career. It was by far his most successful work of fiction as measured by copies sold. A list of the estimated sales of his books in his lifetime in Britain and America gives a figure of 'above 30,000' for 'Daisy Miller', and the next highest is a mere 13,500 for *The Portrait of a Lady*.[1] It was the closest James came to writing a 'bestseller', though it predated the coinage of that word, and unfortunately he did not reap the monetary reward it usually implies. In those days it was necessary to publish a book in America, if only a few copies, to establish the author's copyright there, and James was too slow to prevent 'Daisy Miller' from being pirated on a large scale before Harper published it in New York as a pamphlet in their 'Half-Hour Series'. That edition sold 20,000 copies in a few weeks, but at a very low royalty-rate. In the summer of 1879 James wrote from England to his friend the novelist and man-of-letters William Dean Howells, who had reported the fame of his story in America: 'Your account of the vogue of *D.M*. . . . embittered my spirit when I reflected that it had awakened no echo (to speak of) in my pocket. I have made 200$ by the whole American career of D.M. . . .'[2]

Nevertheless the literary status and celebrity James acquired from 'Daisy Miller', on both sides of the Atlantic, was a priceless

asset. It is not an exaggeration to say that this modestly pro-
portioned work, short enough to be read comfortably at a single
sitting (though perhaps not, with appreciation, in half an hour),
was the foundation of his distinguished subsequent career. Dis-
cerning readers had perceived the promise of his earlier fiction
– the novels *Roderick Hudson* (1875) and *The American*
(1877), and stories like 'Madame de Mauves' (1874) – but it
was 'Daisy Miller' which really impressed his name on the
collective consciousness of the English and American reading
publics as a new star in the literary firmament, with a distinctive
vision and voice. It was, as he wrote to his mother at the
time, 'a really quite extraordinary hit'.[3] Above all, its success
confirmed for the author himself that, in the social and cultural
interaction of America and Europe, he had found a wonderfully
rich seam of material for fictional exploitation. This is evi-
denced by his quickly following up 'Daisy Miller' with the
slightly longer tale 'An International Episode', serialized in the
winter of 1878–9, which is a kind of reversal of the earlier
one, sending a couple of rather dim upper-class Englishmen to
America with ironic consequences; and then collecting these
two stories, together with 'Four Meetings', the poignant
account of an American schoolmistress's frustrated desire to
see Europe (she gets no further than Le Havre), in a book
published by Macmillan in England in 1879. James consoli-
dated his reputation with *The Portrait of a Lady* (1881), a
full-length novel about a young American heiress 'affronting
her destiny'[4] in Europe, and he continued to compose variations
on the 'international theme' throughout his career, including
his late masterpieces *The Wings of the Dove* (1902), *The
Ambassadors* (1903) and *The Golden Bowl* (1904).

It was subject matter he was uniquely fitted to explore by the
circumstances of his life. He was born in New York in 1843,
the second son in a family of four boys (the eldest of whom,
William James, became an eminent philosopher and psycholo-
gist) and one girl, Alice. Their father, Henry James Sr, was a
man of strong, unorthodox opinions on education, which his
inherited income allowed him to indulge. He believed that his
children would benefit from being exposed to the influence of

European culture from an early age and with this aim took them on frequent extended visits to England and the Continent, where for periods they were put to school. The consequence, especially for the two eldest and most gifted brothers, was a somewhat disjointed education which retarded their discovery of their true vocations, and Henry came to believe that the restless, itinerant nature of his early life had alienated him from his native country and led him to make his literary career in Europe (for a time in France, and then permanently in England, where he settled in 1876). But if some personal and psychological loss was involved in this expatriate existence, there was an immense gain for literature, which 'Daisy Miller' was the first of his works to demonstrate to a large audience.

THE GENESIS OF THE STORY

Every fictional story has its moment of conception, when the basic idea, or 'germ' as Henry James called it, is first planted in the writer's imagination. For James this was something often told to him in casual conversation, as in the case of 'Daisy Miller'. In the Preface to volume XVIII of the New York Edition of *The Novels and Tales of Henry James* (1907–9), which included an extensively revised text of the story some thirty years after its original publication, he recalled:

> It was in Rome during the autumn of 1877; a friend then living there ... happened to mention – which she might perfectly not have done – some simple and uninformed American lady of the previous winter, whose young daughter, a child of nature and of freedom, accompanying her from hotel to hotel, had 'picked up' by the wayside, with the best conscience in the world, a good-looking Roman, of vague identity, astonished at his luck, yet (so far as might be, by the pair) all innocently, all serenely exhibited and introduced: this at least till the occurrence of some small social check, some interrupting incident, of no great gravity or dignity, and which I forget.[5]

Out of this slight, almost trivial, anecdote James wove a story
which dramatizes profound differences of manners between
America and Europe, and more importantly between different
classes of Americans who meet in Europe. For the principal
opposition in the action of 'Daisy Miller' is not between Americans and Europeans (as it was in *The American* for instance)
but between two kinds of Americans in Europe: the upper-class,
regular visitors and residents like Mrs Costello and Mrs
Walker, who scrupulously observe the proprieties of 'good'
society in the Old World (which also serves as their model in
the New), and the less cultivated, more provincial *nouveaux
riches* American tourists, like the Millers, who behave exactly
as they do at home. Henry James was one of the first novelists
to grasp the social significance of tourism, as an activity access-
ible to anyone affluent enough to take advantage of the ease
of travel in the industrial age. In America – certainly in the
'minutely hierarchical' society of New York (17) – the snobbish
Costellos and Walkers would have avoided any social contact
with the Millers; in Europe, however, the latter must be either
assimilated or ostentatiously excluded. Mrs Costello, who
defines herself as 'very exclusive' (16) and is naively admired
by Daisy for that attribute (20), is determined to exclude the
Millers from the beginning: 'They are very common . . . They
are the sort of Americans that one does one's duty by not – not
accepting' (17). Mrs Walker offers Daisy the opportunity to be
assimilated, but is rebuffed, with fatal consequences. It is the
European context which raises the stakes in this conflict of
manners, and at the centre of the conflict, trying to interpret it,
taking part in it, and having a personal interest in the outcome,
is a young man who is American by birth but has lived most of
his life in Europe, and does not fully belong to either society:
Winterbourne. There was no such person in the anecdote which
provided James with his 'germ'; he is entirely James's invention,
and a crucial one, for the story is as much about Winterbourne
as it is about Daisy Miller.

James also added to his source-story an earlier episode in a
different setting: Winterbourne first meets Daisy Miller in the
little resort of Vevey on the shores of Lake Geneva, and is both

charmed and confused by her uninhibited friendliness, while his aunt is scandalized by her readiness to make an excursion with him to the Castle of Chillon. When Winterbourne catches up with Daisy in Rome some months later, he is disconcerted to find that she has acquired an Italian escort, Mr Giovanelli, a handsome young man of dubious social status, thought to be a fortune-hunter, whom she insists on introducing to the exclusive circle presided over by Winterbourne's friend, Mrs Walker. The way Daisy conducts herself with this admirer without apparently being engaged to him causes her to be ostracized by Mrs Walker's set, to which Daisy responds by flouting the conventions still more openly. When Winterbourne encounters her alone with Giovanelli in the Colosseum by moonlight, he finally decides that 'She was a young lady whom a gentleman need no longer be at pains to respect' (59–60). Daisy catches the 'Roman fever' (malaria) as a result of this rash adventure and dies shortly afterwards.

MANNERS

'Daisy Miller' begins as a comedy of manners and ends as a tragedy of manners. As James himself said to a correspondent two years after its first publication, 'The whole idea of the story is the little tragedy of a light, thin, natural, unsuspecting creature being sacrificed, as it were, to a social rumpus that went on quite over her head & to which she stood in no measurable relation.'[6] It may be difficult for readers in the twenty-first century to understand that a rumpus about manners could have such grave consequences, but in the nineteenth century 'manners' in the sense of 'external social behaviour' still retained some of the older meaning of 'morals'. The conduct of Daisy and her family violates the code of manners to which Mrs Costello and Mrs Walker subscribe in several ways, some of which are explicitly noted, others merely implied in the narrative. The Millers are, for instance, much too familiar with their courier, transgressing the order of the European class-system. They do not conform to the authoritarian structure of the traditional patriarchal family: Mr Miller is at home in Schenectady, earning the money that sends his womenfolk unprotected to Europe, and Mrs Miller is a weak, unintelligent mother, unable to counsel her daughter or control her obstreperous young son. They are largely ignorant of European culture and history, and their speech lacks elegance and polish. The main issue, however, on which the whole story turns, is the proper conduct of a young unmarried woman in relation to the opposite sex.

At the time and place in which the story is set a respectable unmarried young lady was not supposed to be in the company of a man without the presence of a chaperone. The unspoken reason for this rule was to guarantee the woman's virginity when she married. The code was therefore inherently sexist and implied a 'double standard' of sexual morality, assuming that men were irrepressible sexual predators who could only be prevented from seducing every available virgin by the watchful guardianship of older women. In practice a young woman could forfeit respectability merely by violating the rule, even if nobody really suspected her of having illicit sexual intercourse. This code was enforced with varying degrees of rigidity in different classes and contexts. In the upper echelons of European society, where marriages were contracts involving the redistribution of inherited wealth and property, and the perpetuation of perhaps historic family names, the guaranteed purity of brides was a high priority and the observance of the code correspondingly strict; but in the more democratic and less cynical society of America the rules were more relaxed. In 'Lady Barberina' (1884), a story Henry James wrote a few years after 'Daisy Miller', a rich young American doctor is attracted by the beautiful daughter of an English aristocratic family but is baffled by the difficulty of getting to know her before asking for her hand in marriage (and, indeed, even after doing so). Having managed to take her aside at a party, he says:

'How do people who marry in England ever know each other before marriage? They have no chance.'

'I am sure I don't know,' said Lady Barberina. 'I never was married.'

'It's very different in my country. There a man may see much of a girl; he may come and see her, he may be constantly alone with her. I wish you allowed that over here.'[7]

Daisy Miller has obviously enjoyed such freedom, as she makes clear to Winterbourne in their first conversation:

'In New York I had lots of society. Last winter I had seventeen dinners given me; and three of them were by gentlemen,' added Daisy Miller . . . she was looking at Winterbourne with all her prettiness in her lively eyes and in her light, slightly monotonous smile. 'I have always had,' she said, 'a great deal of gentlemen's society.' (11)

By delaying Daisy's final declarative sentence with a description of her attractive appearance, and then delaying its conclusion further with the inserted speech tag 'she said', James makes us feel its effect on the young man before he tells us: 'Poor Winterbourne was amused, perplexed, and decidedly charmed.' Winterbourne does not know how to interpret the manners of this young woman from Schenectady. He has 'never yet heard a young girl express herself in just this fashion' except where it revealed 'a certain laxity of deportment'.

Was she simply a pretty girl from New York State – were they all like that, the pretty girls who had a good deal of gentlemen's society? Or was she also a designing, an audacious, an unscrupulous young person? (12)

This is the question that torments Winterbourne for the duration of his acquaintance with Daisy. Is she a new type of fearless, independent but virtuous American womanhood, or is she a shameless coquette who exploits the relative freedom apparently permitted to young people in America? His aunt tells him he is unqualified to judge correctly.

'You have lived too long out of the country. You will be sure to make some great mistake. You are too innocent.'

'My dear aunt, I am not so innocent,' said Winterbourne, smiling and curling his moustache. (18)

Moustaches are a physical index of male sexual maturity and function in this story as metonymic symbols of virility (Winterbourne is jealous when he discovers Daisy in Rome 'surrounded by half-a-dozen wonderful moustaches' (33); so, in curling his moustache as he denies being 'innocent', he is hinting (or pretending) that he is sexually experienced – enough, at least, to judge whether Daisy is morally 'innocent'. But in fact he cannot make up his mind about her behaviour, much to his own annoyance. Not until his final encounter with Daisy, in the Colosseum, does he condemn her unequivocally – only to discover later that he was mistaken. (He has in fact made precisely the opposite 'great mistake', as Millicent Bell observes, to the one his aunt predicted.)[8] At Daisy's funeral Giovanelli assures him that she was 'the most innocent' young lady he had ever known, and Winterbourne realizes, too late, that she might have returned his love – or as he puts it to his aunt, in his prim way, 'She would have appreciated one's esteem' (63, 64).

THE POINT OF VIEW

Henry James was one of the first writers to grasp, theoretically as well as intuitively, the importance of 'point of view' in telling a story. From whose perspective should it be told – one character's, several characters', the omniscient author's or a combination of these methods (as in the classic Victorian novel)? This fundamental choice by the writer will determine the meaning and effect of any story. 'Daisy Miller' is an early example of James's mastery of the single, limited and fallible point of view. The title implies that Daisy is the subject of the tale, but everything we, as readers, know about her is filtered through the consciousness of Winterbourne. We only see her through his eyes; we only acquire information about her that is passed to him. Therefore, in making up our own minds about Daisy's character we are simultaneously having to make up our minds about Winterbourne's, and about the reliability of his perceptions and judgments.

There is an authorial narrator, who on a few occasions refers to himself as 'I'. He sets the scene at the opening of the story and conveys certain facts about Winterbourne (though never directly about Daisy); but for the most part his persona is unobtrusive and self-effacing, very unlike the expansive, judgmental authorial narrators of, say, Dickens's novels, or George Eliot's. Many of Winterbourne's private thoughts about Daisy are rendered in free indirect style, transposing what he is saying to himself, or asking himself, into a third-person/past-tense discourse, but preserving his diction, so that we have the illusion of direct access to his mind. An example would be the sentence just quoted above: 'Was she simply a pretty girl from New York State – were they all like that, the pretty girls who had a good deal of gentlemen's society?' Even when his thoughts are reported in a more straightforward way, there is so little difference between the style of the authorial voice and that of Winterbourne's own speech that we have very little sense of moving outside his consciousness. To take an example from the same place, in 'Poor Winterbourne was amused, perplexed, and decidedly charmed' the authorial epithet, 'Poor', expresses an amused sympathy with the young man's bafflement rather than ironic detachment, and the other words are exactly those he would have used about himself.

This authorial narrator is certainly not omniscient. 'I hardly know,' he says, after the opening description of Vevey, comparing its hotels to those of American resorts, 'whether it was the analogies or the differences that were uppermost in the mind of a young American, who, two or three years ago, sat in the garden of the "Trois Couronnes" . . .' (4). The narrator tells us very little about the background and past history of this young man, and the most interesting information is notably ambiguous:

when certain persons spoke of him they affirmed that the reason of his spending so much time at Geneva was that he was extremely devoted to a lady who lived there – a foreign lady – a person older than himself. Very few Americans – indeed I think none – had ever seen this lady, about whom there were some singular stories. (4)

The ambiguity is, pointedly, never resolved. At the end of the story Winterbourne returns to live in Geneva, 'whence there continue to come the most contradictory accounts of his motives of sojourn: a report that he is "studying" hard – an intimation that he is much interested in a very clever foreign lady' (64).

WINTERBOURNE AND WOMEN; JAMES AND WOMEN

Since Winterbourne's interest in Daisy is at least partly sexual, the question of his own sexuality is highly relevant to our interpretation of his speculations about Daisy's character. His surname, by which the narrator always refers to him – only twice is his Christian name, Frederick, used, when his aunt addresses him (17, 19)[9] – suggests 'born of winter', or one who has a wintry life ahead of him ('bourn' being an archaic word for destination). This discourages us from believing that he is conducting a passionate love affair in Geneva, and his general behaviour, thoughts and speech present him as a young man who, though superficially sophisticated, is in fact sexually diffident and probably inexperienced. He is attracted to Daisy's pretty looks and vitality at their first meeting and he is excited by her availability, living as he does in a society where 'nice' girls are unapproachable except under very strict surveillance. When she invites him on the spur of the moment to take her out on the lake in a boat at night he begs her mother 'ardently' to let her go, for 'he had never yet enjoyed the sensation of guiding through the summer starlight a skiff freighted with a fresh and beautiful young girl' (25). But the appearance of the courier puts paid to this scheme. 'I hope you are disappointed, or disgusted, or something!' she says skittishly, bidding him goodnight. Winterbourne says only, 'I am puzzled.'

> He lingered beside the lake for a quarter of an hour, turning over the mystery of the young girl's sudden familiarities and caprices. But the only very definite conclusion he came to was that he should enjoy deucedly 'going off' with her somewhere. (27)

He manages to take Daisy to Chillon unchaperoned, and as she comes down the stairs to meet him 'he felt as if there were something romantic going forward' and 'could have believed he was going to elope with her' (27); but he is so preoccupied with observing and analysing her behaviour on the trip that he doesn't fully enjoy her company – at least, Daisy asks him, 'What on *earth* are you so grave about? ... You look as if you were taking me to a funeral' (28). When he tells her that he must leave Vevey and return to Geneva the next day, she expresses her disappointment so emphatically that 'Poor Winterbourne was fairly bewildered; no young lady had as yet done him the honour to be so agitated by the announcement of his movements' (30). The prissy diction here betrays a certain alarm that Daisy is forcing the pace of their relationship. As she accuses him of being in thrall to some female 'charmer' in Geneva (whose existence he denies), she seems to him 'an extraordinary mixture of innocence and crudity' (30). Later, in Rome, her conduct with Giovanelli strikes him as 'an inscrutable combination of audacity and innocence' (41). Is she really 'nice' or a coquette? Is her 'flirting' harmless or dangerous? Should he court her with respect, or 'treat her as the object of one of those sentiments which are called by romancers "lawless passions"' (41)? He ends up doing neither, because of

> his want of instinctive certitude as to how far her eccentricities were generic, national, and how far they were personal. From either view of them he had somehow missed her, and now it was too late. She was 'carried away' by Mr. Giovanelli. (56)

The discomfort of his situation, tugged back and forth by conflicting loyalties to both sides in the war of manners, is subtly dramatized in the sequence when he escorts Daisy to the Pincio gardens. Having given her his protection through the Roman streets, he is obliged to hand her over to a rival whom he suspects and despises; then, when Daisy refuses Mrs Walker's insistent invitation to get into her carriage, Winterbourne is ignominiously compelled to get in himself, under the threat of banishment if he does not, and to watch Daisy walk away with Giovanelli. When he gets out of the carriage and goes in pursuit of Daisy and 'her cavalier', the intimacy of their posture, half concealed by a parasol, stops him in his tracks, and he walks – 'not towards the couple with the parasol; towards the residence of his aunt, Mrs. Costello' (46).

Winterbourne is one of several young men in James's early novels and stories who are attracted to certain women but restrained by various doubts and inhibitions from seeking a permanent relationship with them, and are left at the end of the story with no prospect of any other. The American hero of 'Madame de Mauves', for instance, Longmore (a name as obviously symbolic as Winterbourne), falls in love with the unhappily married eponymous heroine (another American expatriate) and is encouraged by her cynical French husband and sister-in-law to become her lover, but Longmore's moral scruples and Madame de Mauves' perverse devotion to the role of the wronged wife lead him to take the path of renunciation and go back to America. Some time later the husband commits suicide, and Longmore's first instinct is to return to Europe. But, says the narrator in the last words of the story:

> Several years have passed, and he still lingers at home. The truth is, that in the midst of all the ardent tenderness of his memory of Madame de Mauves, he has become conscious of a singular feeling, – a feeling for which awe would be hardly too strong a name.[10]

'Fear' might be too strong, but not altogether wide of the mark. One of the most interesting interpolations of the narrator of

'Daisy Miller' about Winterbourne concerns the latter's puzzled perception of her relaxed and inclusive friendliness:

> He could hardly have said why, but she seemed to him a girl who would never be jealous. At the risk of exciting a somewhat derisive smile on the reader's part, I may affirm that with regard to the women who had hitherto interested him it very often seemed to Winterbourne among the possibilities that, given certain contingencies, he should be afraid – literally afraid – of these ladies. He had a pleasant sense that he should never be afraid of Daisy Miller. (52)

Instead of following up this 'pleasant sense' in order to enjoy Daisy's company more, however, Winterbourne perversely interprets her inclusive friendliness as a sign of moral weakness. The passage continues: 'It must be added that this sentiment was not altogether flattering to Daisy; it was part of his conviction, or rather of his apprehension, that she would prove a very light young person.' So there is a sense in which Winterbourne *is* afraid of Daisy, or at least of the temptation to 'lawless passions' which, in one aspect, she represents for him.

'"Frederick Winterbourne, c'est moi," [Henry James] might have said,' observes a modern critic, echoing Flaubert's famous remark about Madame Bovary.[11] That is probably an overstatement, but it is likely that he put a good deal of himself into the portrayal of Winterbourne and similar characters. It is the view of his most authoritative biographer, Leon Edel, that James both worshipped and feared his mother and that this ambivalence was carried over into his adult relationships with women.[12] He was attracted to many women in his life, and had intimate friendships with several, but he always backed off when there seemed any risk of being drawn into marriage or any kind of sexual relationship. By the mid-1870s, not long before he wrote 'Daisy Miller', he had decided that he would not marry. How far this decision was due to his determination to dedicate himself fully to his art, and how far to a growing awareness of his own ambiguous sexual nature, is hard to say. Edel, and the majority of his other biographers, believe that he never had a physical relationship with anyone of either sex, but in the last analysis they must admit that it is impossible to be certain on such matters and leave further speculation to novelists.[13] What is clear is that he was not a closet gay writer, like, say, E. M. Forster, who had no real interest in heterosexual love and was obliged to fake the representation of it in his fiction. The man who wrote, 'he had never yet enjoyed the sensation of guiding through the summer starlight a skiff freighted with a fresh and beautiful young girl' was not a stranger to 'straight' romantic attraction. Henry James wrote some of the greatest novels in modern literature about love, and the betrayal of love, between men and women, and no one has written better about marriage this side of the bedroom door. But he was also able to draw on his own experience and temperament to create memorable portraits of repression, inhibition, diffidence and regret in the affective life of men like Winterbourne. In a way, these troubled, self-doubting, eternally celibate heroes are surrogates for the writer himself. Like him they observe life rather than participate fully in it, but without enjoying the compensating creative fulfilment of the artist.

WHAT KIND OF 'STUDY'?

When it was first published, 'Daisy Miller' was subtitled 'A Study', an interestingly problematic term. In the late nineteenth century it could mean 'a discourse or literary composition devoted to the detailed consideration of some question, or the minute description of some object' or 'a literary work executed as an exercise or an experiment in some particular style or mode of treatment'. Although these meanings are not entirely irrelevant to 'Daisy Miller', they do not apply exactly. James's subtitle is therefore usually interpreted as a metaphor drawn from the visual arts; but even in that context 'a study' can mean several different things, from 'a careful preliminary sketch for a work of art' or 'an artist's pictorial record of his observation of some object, incident, or effect, or of something that occurs to his mind, intended for his own guidance in his subsequent work' to 'a drawing, painting or piece of sculpture aiming to bring out the characteristics of the object represented, as they are revealed by especially careful observation'.[14] Leon Edel maintains that James was implying by the word 'study' that 'he had written the equivalent of a pencil-sketch on an artist's pad rather than a rounded character'[15] and quotes in support a remark in the Preface to the revised version of the story in the New York Edition of 1909. James dropped the subtitle in this edition and professed not to remember the reasons why he had originally appended it, 'unless they may have taken account simply of a certain flatness in my poor little heroine's literal denomination'.[16] This itself is, however, a somewhat cryptic explanation (it is not obvious that 'Daisy Miller' is a particularly 'flat' name). In any case the Preface is a deceptive guide to the story and needs to be treated with caution. There is an obvious sense in which the last of the dictionary definitions of 'study' cited above is metaphorically applicable to 'Daisy Miller'. As several critics have pointed out, throughout the story Winterbourne is continually, almost obsessively 'studying' Daisy, both as a type and as an individual.[17] He is immediately attracted by her pretty appearance, but his first reaction classifies her generically: '"How pretty they are!" thought Winterbourne, straightening himself in his seat' (6). 'They' means 'American girls', though we are able to infer this only because of the narrator's introductory remarks about the invasion of the Swiss hotel by American tourists, and the 'flitting hither and thither of "stylish" young girls' who make Vevey seem like Newport or Saratoga (3). We are told that Winterbourne 'had a great relish for feminine beauty; he was addicted to observing and analysing it' (8). He soon becomes addicted to observing and analysing every aspect of Daisy's person and behaviour, long after Mrs Walker's circle have made up their minds about her.

> They ceased to invite her, and they intimated that they desired to express to observant Europeans the great truth that, though Miss Daisy Miller was a young American lady, her behaviour was not representative – was regarded by her compatriots as abnormal. (55–6)

On one level – the level of character psychology – Winter-bourne's treatment of Daisy as an object of 'study' is a way of displacing or suppressing his own erotic interest in her. As Philip Horne astutely observes, 'a secure state of knowledge about her even becomes at certain points, perversely, more desirable to him than Daisy's virtue'.[18] But there is no doubt that the anthropological or sociological aspect of the story contributed very largely to its popularity. The question of whether Daisy was an accurate portrait of a recognizable type of young American girl or 'an outrage on American girlhood'[19] and the related question of whether she was an innocent victim of social prejudice or the author of her own misfortunes were fiercely debated, especially in America. W. D. Howells reported to his and James's mutual friend, the writer James Russell Lowell, then resident in England:

> HJ waked up all the women with his *Daisy Miller*, the intention of which they misconceived. And there has been a vast discussion in which nobody felt very deeply, and everybody talked very loudly. The thing went so far that society almost divided itself into Daisy Millerites and anti-Daisy Millerites.[20]

If this suggests a prejudice against James's heroine among genteel American women, there were enough female admirers to make 'Daisy Miller' hats fashionable for a while.[21] In the longer term, 'Daisy Miller' entered the language as a generic term for a certain type of attractive but forward and uncultivated young American girl at large in Europe.

Henry James was not altogether pleased by the proverbial status his creation acquired. It irritated him that throughout his career he was best known and remembered by the general public as the author of this early and comparatively slight work, while his much more ambitious and complex later fictions were neg-lected. His last secretary, Theodora Bosanquet, compared his feelings to those of 'some *grande dame* possessing a jewel-case richly stocked with glowing rubies and flashing diamonds, but condemned by her admirers always to appear in the single string of moonstones worn at her first dance'.[22] This helps to explain the somewhat deprecatory tone of James's remarks about the story in the Preface, and the curious discussion of it with two friends which he claims to have had some time after its original publication. Although there was no doubt a factual basis for this anecdote, one can hardly avoid the conclusion that James improved it in the telling for his own purposes. The three friends are observing the indecorous behaviour of a pair of young American girls on the water-steps of a hotel in Venice, and one describes them as 'a couple of attesting Daisy Millers' (meaning that they prove the representativeness of James's character). The other companion, his 'hostess', protests against this application of the name and then addresses the author in a long speech of such syntactical and rhetorical complexity, flattering him under the appearance of chiding him, that only Henry James himself could have composed it, and no human being could possibly have recalled it verbatim after an interval of years. The essential gist of her accusation is that James, having started out with a character who was a recognizable and generally deplorable 'type', invested her with such irresistible charm and pathos as to make her quite exceptional, so that paradoxically the two young Americans 'capering' before them are the 'real little Daisy Millers' while James's heroine is not. James meekly concedes that 'my supposedly typical little figure was of course pure poetry, and had never been anything else . . .' (see Appendix I: Preface to the New York Edition, below, p. 67).

By this devious means Henry James sought to correct the received view of 'Daisy Miller' as a realistic 'study' of a certain kind of young American woman and to present it as a work of imagination which transcends the limits of empirical verisimilitude. At the time when the story originally appeared, James was often linked with Howells as an exponent of a new kind of social realism in post-Civil War American fiction, but it was a classification that proved less and less appropriate as his work developed. The 'solidity of specification' which characterized his earlier novels and tales, and which he still insisted was an essential requirement of the 'Art of Fiction', in his 1884 essay of that title,[23] gave way to a more impressionistic, ambiguous and subjective rendering of experience in the later ones. In the

late 1890s and the early years of the twentieth century James's
fiction took a direction that could indeed be described as
'poetic', entailing the use of iterative symbolism and a highly
wrought style permeated with metaphor. The very titles of some
of the key works of his 'major phase' – 'The Turn of the Screw',
The Wings of the Dove, *The Golden Bowl*, 'The Beast in the
Jungle' – illustrate the point, contrasting with the simple refer-
ential titles characteristic of the earlier ones: *Roderick Hudson*,
The American, 'Madame de Mauves', 'Daisy Miller'. In the
1909 Preface, therefore, James was trying to present 'Daisy
Miller' as a kind of minor precursor of his mature art, playing
down the very qualities that had made it so popular on its first
appearance. And the changes and additions he made to the
text in the 1909 version were, consciously or unconsciously,
motivated by a desire to make it (as far as was possible without
completely rewriting it) stylistically consistent with his later
work, and to encourage a view of the heroine as exceptional
rather than typical.

STYLE: THE TWO TEXTS

It has been estimated that James modified ninety per cent of the
sentences of the original text in the New York Edition and
added some fifteen per cent to its length.[24] Many of the revisions
are trivial, and none of them alters the structure of the story;
but cumulatively they have a considerable effect on the way
the reader receives it. The most significant fall into one of
three categories: (1) expanded descriptions of Winterbourne's
thoughts about Daisy; (2) the replacement of simple speech-
tags, like 'he/she said/declared/exclaimed' with more elabor-
ately descriptive phrases (which also reflect Winterbourne's
perceptions); and more rarely, (3) emendations of the dialogue
itself, which generally add emphasis rather than changing the
original meanings. The 1909 text contains more information
than the 1879 text, but because this additional information is
nearly all about Winterbourne (since nearly everything is narrated from his point of view) it actually unbalances the story,

in the present editor's opinion, and spoils the quality which
W. D. Howells very perceptively singled out for special praise,
when he wrote to James in 1882, three years after its first
publication: 'That artistic impartiality which puzzled so many
in the treatment of Daisy Miller is one of the qualities most
valuable in the eyes of those who care how things are done . . .
this impartiality comes at last to the same result as sympathy.'[25]
What Howells meant by 'artistic impartiality' was James's
refusal to judge his heroine. Instead, he shows Winterbourne
judging her, and leaves it to the reader to decide how justly.
Judging Daisy entails judging Winterbourne; this complicates
the interpretative process and involves the reader in the active
'production' of the text in a way more characteristic of modern
fiction than the classic Victorian novel. Both versions of the
story make this demand on the reader, but in the 1909 text the
disparity between the 'objective' reality of Daisy and Winterbourne's subjective responses to her, between the transparency
of her speech and the 'logic-chopping' (56) complexity of his
inner dialogue with himself, is more marked and insistent.
Philip Horne, who has made a scrupulous comparison of the
two texts, observes that, 'whereas the first edition offers strong
intermittent hints that we should doubt Winterbourne's con-
clusions, the NYE works the doubts far more closely into the
texture of the narration', and 'in the revised version the speeches
stand out from the interpretative framework Winterbourne
progressively tries to fit them into'.[26] By making us, as readers,
less likely to trust Winterbourne, the 1909 text correspondingly
makes us more likely to sympathize with Daisy, but, as Howells
observed, the 'impartiality' of the 1879 text is not incompatible
with 'sympathy' for her; it merely makes the reader work harder
to achieve it. The impartiality also extends to the characterization of Winterbourne, generating more sympathy for him than
he seems to deserve in the 1909 version, so that we end the
story with a feeling of regret for his unfulfilled life as well as
sadness at the untimely end of Daisy's.

   Although the 1879 text is shorter, sparer and stylistically
simpler than the 1909 text it is paradoxically richer in meaning
– but the meaning inheres as much in what is implied as in what

is stated. One might almost say that in 'Daisy Miller' James anticipated Ernest Hemingway's theory of the short story: that 'you could omit anything if you knew what you omitted, and the omitted part would strengthen the story and make people feel something more than they understood'.[27] Indeed William James (often a severe critic of his brother's work) praised another, earlier story of Henry's in precisely those terms: 'You expressly restrict yourself, accordingly, to showing a few external acts and speeches, and by the magic of your art making the reader *feel* back of these the existence of a body of being of which these are casual features.'[28] Not a word in 'Daisy Miller' is redundant. Where there is repetition, the repetition is functional (notably in the artless speech of the Miller family, whose members characteristically employ the same keyword or phrase again and again, contrasting with the elegant variation in the Europeanized characters' dialogue), and the silences are eloquent. Comparison with the revised text helps to bring out the qualities of the original story.

Consider, for example, the first scene. 'Scene' is a particularly appropriate term because the whole story unfolds in a sequence of dramatic encounters between the characters as they might be presented in a good play or film, where every line of dialogue (however banal), every bit of body language, every glance and pause, signifies. 'Dramatize, dramatize!' was James's watchword, according to the Preface, long before he attempted to make himself a playwright, and he was always much more successful in applying the lessons of drama to narrative than he was in writing for performance (including his adaptation of 'Daisy Miller' for the stage).[29] Winterbourne is seated on the terrace of the hotel, enjoying a coffee and a cigarette, when he is accosted by young Randolph Miller, asking for a lump of sugar from his table (for the quotations below see pp. 5–7). Randolph, who was not in James's source-anecdote, is a brilliant comic creation. He is a little American barbarian, who affronts European standards of decorum in both speech and behaviour much more blatantly than his sister or mother – refusing to go to bed at an appropriate hour, eating what he fancies, doing what he likes, despising Europe and boasting about his native country; but he does it all with such self-assurance and amusing candour, combining youthful indiscretion with a certain knowingness, that he functions in the story as a kind of jester or wise fool, exposing the tensions and contradictions in the adult social context. In this first scene, he takes three lumps of sugar from Winterbourne and bites one of them: '"Oh, blazes; it's har-r-d!" he exclaimed, pronouncing the adjective in a peculiar manner.' The 1909 text reads as follows: '"Oh, blazes; it's har-r-d!" he exclaimed, divesting vowel and consonants, pertinently enough, of any taint of softness.'

The verbal phrase in the second version is stylistically typical of late James, playing on the word 'hard' and opposing it to 'softness' (he loved figures of antithesis) and using muted metaphor in 'divesting' and 'taint'; but one has to ask whether this rhetorical flourish serves any purpose other than to emphasize the obvious cultural distance between Winterbourne and Randolph, and to make the former seem rather too pleased with his own wit. In the original text he is much more interested in the boy. 'Peculiar' there has the meaning of 'distinctive' and leads more logically to the next sentence, which is almost the same in both versions: 'Winterbourne had immediately perceived that he might have the honour of claiming him as a fellow-countryman ['countryman' in 1909]'. There follows a droll speech from Randolph in which he blames the chronic loss of his milk-teeth on Europe and its hotels, and then a conversation about the relative merits of American and European candy, boys – and men. 'Are you an American man?' Randolph asks. On receiving an affirmative answer, 'American men are the best,' he declares ('with assurance' the 1909 version redundantly adds), and then, 'Here comes my sister! . . . She's an American girl.' To which Winterbourne, seeing a beautiful young lady advancing, 'cheerfully' replies: 'American girls are the best girls.' Because Winterbourne has to adopt the simple directness of the child's speech, the conversation highlights issues which will be crucial to the story. Is Winterbourne a real American? Is he a real man? Is Daisy the best kind of girl?

The first encounter between Winterbourne and Daisy is

beautifully handled and full of subtle implication. We sense Winterbourne's immediate interest in and attraction to her, and also his uncertainty about how to proceed. He is constrained by a code of manners which requires a man to be introduced to a lady before he speaks to her; according to the same code, Daisy should either find a gracious way of overcoming this difficulty, perhaps by employing Randolph, or remove herself and her brother promptly from the stranger's presence, but Daisy seems disinclined to either course of action. She reproves Randolph for scattering the pebbles around Winterbourne's ears without acknowledging the young man's existence at all. Winterbourne addresses a remark to Randolph, who tells his sister, 'He's an American man!' but 'The young lady gave no heed to this announcement' (the 1909 text has 'this circumstance', which is weaker, departing from the 'introduction' subtext). ' "Well, I guess you had better be quiet," she simply observed.' Winterbourne then presumes to treat Randolph's remark as an introduction and addresses Daisy directly. She glances at him but says nothing and looks over the parapet at the lake and the mountains.

> While he was thinking of something else to say, the young lady turned to the little boy again.
>   'I should like to know where you got that pole,' she said.

The 1909 text has '. . . the young lady turned again to the little boy, whom she addressed quite as if they were alone together'. The additional clause is not really necessary, and indeed the scene works much better if we sense the unconventionality of her behaviour without having the reasons spelled out. Such changes are quite small-scale, but they have a cumulative effect, and further on in the scene there are more substantial revisions which would take too long to analyse here. (The Note on the Text below has further discussion of the revisions in the 1909 edition.) I have tried to illustrate with this brief example how the surface simplicity and economy of the story's style and narrative method actually generate a great density of meaning and implication. These qualities are by no means completely effaced in the New York Edition, but they are more consistently present in the original text, right up to its beautifully understated conclusion.

CONCLUSION

Imagine what a sentimental meal a Victorian novelist would have made of Daisy Miller's last illness! There are no deathbed histrionics in this story. Winterbourne never sees Daisy after the scene in the Colosseum, and James conveys the pathos and finality of her death by the almost brutal brevity with which he reports it, 'cutting' (like a film-maker) quickly to the funeral. Daisy sends him a message through her mother to say that she was not engaged to Giovanelli:

'I don't know why she wanted you to know; but she said to me three times – "Mind you tell Mr. Winterbourne." And then she told me to ask if you remembered the time you went to that castle, in Switzerland. But I said I wouldn't give any such messages as that. Only, if she is not engaged, I'm sure I'm glad to know it.'

But, as Winterbourne had said, it mattered very little. A week after this the poor girl died; it had been a terrible case of the fever. Daisy's grave was in the little Protestant cemetery ... (62–3)

The phrase 'it mattered very little' is not quite as callous as it sounds out of context. It takes us back by a direct echo to the climactic scene in the Colosseum. As Giovanelli goes off to see to the carriage, Daisy chatters defiantly about the beauty of the scene. When she wonders why he is silent he merely laughs, and she asks: '*Did* you believe I was engaged the other day?'

'It doesn't matter what I believed the other day,' said Winterbourne, still laughing.

'Well, what do you believe now?'

'I believe it makes very little difference whether you are engaged or not!' (61)

There is a double implication here: that if Daisy were engaged
to Giovanelli it would not affect the impropriety of her being
alone with him at that hour in such a place, and that for the
same reason Winterbourne is no longer interested in whether
her affections are engaged or not. He is in a state of shock, and
we may feel that there is a touch of hysteria about his laughter.
But of course the question *does* matter to Daisy, because she
really cares for him, as she later reveals by the message she
sends him through her mother.

The sentence 'But, as Winterbourne had said, it mattered
very little' is charged with emotions carried over from the
previous scene. The 1909 text, 'But as Winterbourne had originally judged, the truth on this question had small actual rel-
evance', contains the same information, but loses the echo of
the dialogue in the Colosseum, and makes Winterbourne sound
coldly forensic – assuming we attribute this reflection to him
rather than to the narrator. It is in fact hard to distinguish
between the two in either version. We can but guess at the
conflicting emotions Winterbourne must be feeling about
Daisy's death. Only after the funeral, when Giovanelli assures
him that Daisy really was 'innocent', and that he had no hope
of marrying her, do they resolve themselves into real grief and
regret:

> 'Why the devil,' he asked, 'did you take her to that fatal place?'
>   Mr. Giovanelli's urbanity was apparently imperturbable. He
> looked on the ground a moment, and then he said, 'For myself,
> I had no fear; and she wanted to go.' (63)

Although Winterbourne is aware of the danger of the Colosseum's unhealthy atmosphere, he lingers there without ill consequences after seeing Daisy with Giovanelli, who for his part
considers himself immune to the 'Roman fever'. In the story
the fever is represented as a lethal threat exclusively to Daisy.
It operates as a symbol, or what T. S. Eliot called an 'objective
correlative',[30] of Daisy's jeopardy as a woman who refuses to
abide by the rules, designed for her protection, of the society in
which she finds herself. Because Daisy merely claims the kind

of freedom that a young woman today would take for granted, it is tempting to regard her as a kind of proto-feminist heroine, defying patriarchal society, but there is nothing ideological in her rebellion against the stuffy ethos of the Mrs Walkers and Mrs Costellos. On the other hand it would be a great mistake to interpret the fever as some kind of providential punishment or poetic justice for misbehaviour. Daisy is indeed partly responsible for her own fate by recklessly ignoring warnings about the fever; but it is the disapproval of the Europeanized Americans, and Winterbourne's chilly reserve in Rome, that push her into more and more extreme demonstrations of her independence and of her determination to enjoy herself, culminating in the fatal visit to the Colosseum. Henry James's comments about Daisy's motivation, a year after the story's first appearance in a letter already quoted,[31] make this clear – indeed, almost too clear. There is a danger that we will take that document as the last, authoritative word on the story. But James was careful to qualify his analysis of Daisy with the parenthesis '(as I understand her)', implying the possibility of understanding her differently. Certainly the narrative method he used so skilfully in the story allows for a wide range of emphases in its interpretation, and makes it infinitely rereadable.

David Lodge

NOTES

1. Graham Clarke, ed., *Henry James: Critical Assessments*. I: *Memories, Views and Writers* (Mountfield: Helm Information, 1991), p. 41.
2. Horne, p. 111.
3. Edel, *Henry James: Letters*, vol. 2, p. 213.
4. Henry James, *The Portrait of a Lady* (Oxford: Oxford University Press, 1962), p. xx.
5. Preface to the New York Edition of *The Novels and Tales of Henry James*, vol. 18 (1909). See Appendix I, below, p. 65.
6. See the letter to Mrs Eliza Lynn Linton in Appendix I, below, p. 71.

7. Henry James, *Collected Stories*, selected and introduced by John Bayley (London: Everyman's Library, 1999), vol. 1, p. 661.
8. Millicent Bell, *Meaning in Henry James* (Cambridge, Mass.: Harvard University Press, 1991), p. 65.
9. In the New York Edition text he introduces himself to Daisy and her mother in Section II as 'Mr. Frederick Forsythe Winterbourne'.
10. *Collected Stories*, vol. 1, p. 258.
11. Vivian R. Pollack, ed., *New Essays on Daisy Miller and The Turn of the Screw* (Cambridge: Cambridge University Press, 1993), Editor's Introduction, p. 5.
12. Leon Edel, *The Life of Henry James* (Harmondsworth: Penguin, 1977), vol. 1, pp. 47–9.
13. See David Lodge, *Author, Author* (London: Secker and Warburg, 2004) and Cólm Toíbin, *The Master* (London: Picador, 2004).
14. All definitions are from the *Oxford English Dictionary*, CD-Rom version 3.1, 2nd edn (2004).
15. Edel, *The Life of Henry James*, vol. 1, p. 517.
16. See the Preface, Appendix I, below, p. 66.
17. For example, Philip Horne, *Henry James and Revision: The New York Edition* (Oxford: Clarendon Press, 1990).
18. Ibid., p. 235.
19. The words are those of Leslie Stephen, quoted by Edel, *The Life of Henry James*, vol. 1, p. 516. James recounts in the Preface that he first submitted the story to the editor of *Lippincott's Magazine*, based in Philadelphia, who promptly rejected it without explanation, and a 'friend' (actually Leslie Stephen, who accepted it for the English *Cornhill Magazine*) suggested that this was the reason.
20. Gard, p. 74.
21. Edel, *The Life of Henry James*, vol. 1, p. 521.
22. Quoted by Jean Gooder, ed., *Henry James: Daisy Miller and Other Stories* (Oxford: Oxford University Press, 1985), p. xiv.
23. Henry James, *The Future of the Novel: Essays on the Art of Fiction*, ed. Leon Edel (New York: Vintage Books, 1956), p. 14.
24. Gooder, *Henry James*, p. xxix. She does not give a source for this information.
25. Quoted by Horne, *Henry James and Revision*, p. 264.
26. Ibid., pp. 234 and 258.
27. William Carlos Baker, *Ernest Hemingway* (Harmondsworth: Penguin, 1972), p. 165.
28. Quoted by Horne, *Henry James and Revision*, p. 229. William

James was commenting on the story 'A Most Extraordinary Case,' first published in 1868.

29. See 'The Play of *Daisy Miller*', Appendix II, below, pp. 73–5.

30. 'The only way of expressing emotion in the form of art is by finding an "objective correlative"; in other words, a set of objects, a situation, a chain of events which shall be the formula of that *particular* emotion . . .' T. S. Eliot, *Selected Essays* (London: Faber and Faber, 1951), p. 145.

31. See note 6 above, and the letter to Mrs. Eliza Lynn Linton, Appendix I, pp. 70–71.

Further Reading

BY HENRY JAMES

Autobiography, ed. Frederick V. Dupee (Princeton, NJ: Princeton University Press, 1983).

The Complete Letters of Henry James, ed. Pierre A. Walker and Greg Zacharias (Nebraska: University of Nebraska Press, 2006–).

The Complete Notebooks, ed. Leon Edel and Lyall H. Powers (New York and Oxford: Oxford University Press, 1987).

The Complete Plays of Henry James, ed. Leon Edel (London: Rupert Hart-Davis, 1949).

Complete Stories, 5 vols. (New York and Cambridge: Library of America, 1996–9).

Henry James: Letters, ed. Leon Edel, 4 vols. (Cambridge, MA.: Belknap Press, 1974–84).

Henry James: A Life in Letters, ed. Philip Horne (London: Penguin, 1999).

The Letters of Henry James, ed. Percy Lubbock, 2 vols. (London, 1920).

Literary Criticism, ed. Leon Edel and Mark Wilson, 2 vols. (New York and Cambridge: Library of America, 1984).

BIOGRAPHY, CRITICISM AND REFERENCE

Edel, Leon, *Henry James: A Life* (New York: Harper & Row, 1985).

Edel, Leon, and Laurence, Dan H., *A Bibliography of Henry*

James, third edn revised with the assistance of James Rambeau (Oxford: Oxford University Press, 1982).

Gard, Roger, ed., *Henry James: The Critical Heritage* (London: Routledge & Kegan Paul, 1968). Contains a very full selection of contemporary reviews and comments.

Graham, Kenneth, *Henry James: A Literary Life* (Basingstoke: Macmillan, 1995).

Kaplan, Fred, *Henry James: The Imagination of Genius* (London: Hodder & Stoughton, 1992).

Nowell-Smith, Simon (compiler), *The Legend of the Master* (London: Constable, 1947).

CRITICISM WITH MATERIAL RELEVANT TO 'DAISY MILLER'

Albers, Christina E., *A Reader's Guide to the Short Stories of Henry James* (New York: G. K. Hall; London: Prentice Hall International, 1997).

Bell, Millicent, *Meaning in Henry James* (Cambridge, Mass.: Harvard University Press, 1991).

Fowler, Virginia C., *Henry James's American Girl* (Madison: University of Wisconsin Press, 1984).

Freedman, Jonathan, *The Cambridge Companion to Henry James* (Cambridge: Cambridge University Press, 1994).

Hayes, Kevin J., ed., *Henry James: The Contemporary Reviews* (Cambridge: Cambridge University Press, 1996).

Hocks, Richard A., *Henry James: A Study of the Short Fiction* (Boston: Twayne, 1990).

Horne, Philip, *Henry James and Revision: The New York Edition* (Oxford: Clarendon Press, 1990).

Pollack, Vivian R., ed., *New Essays on Daisy Miller and The Turn of the Screw* (Cambridge: Cambridge University Press, 1993).

D.L.

A Note on the Text

'Daisy Miller: A Study' first appeared as a two-part serial in the English *Cornhill Magazine*, edited by Leslie Stephen, in June and July 1878. It was published as a pamphlet by Harper in New York, in November of that year, no. 82 of their 'Half-Hour Series'. In 1879 it was published by Macmillan in London as the title story of a book that also included 'An International Episode' and 'Four Meetings'. 'Daisy Miller' was reprinted in volume 13 of the 'Collective Edition' of James's fiction brought out by Macmillan in 1883, with a few insignificant differences in the text from the 1879 edition. In 1909 *Daisy Miller* was included in volume 18 of the massive New York Edition of *The Novels and Tales of Henry James* issued by Scribner's (New York) and Macmillan (London) between 1907 and 1909. Henry James took the opportunity to revise the texts for this edition, and his revisions were particularly extensive in the case of 'Daisy Miller'.

Whether James was well advised to undertake the revision of his earlier work in general, and of 'Daisy Miller' in particular, are matters of considerable disagreement among scholars and critics. This Penguin edition is based on the text of the first English publication in book form, by Macmillan in 1879 – an editorial choice made for two reasons. Firstly, the original story is a fine example of James's fiction at the time he wrote it, and for readers interested in tracing his artistic development it is the only useful text. The 1909 text is a hybrid of James's earlier and later styles, however artfully blended. Secondly, as I indicated in the Introduction, in my opinion the earlier version is superior as a work of literature to the later. Other scholars and editors have taken a contrary view. John Lyon, for instance, who reprinted the 1909 text of 'Daisy Miller' in an earlier Penguin Classics edition of *Selected Tales* by Henry James (2001), declared that 'Jamesian revision is overwhelmingly improvement; he did *not* convert earlier lucidities into what some feel to be the indirect obscurities of the later style; and indeed, many of the revisions serve greater precision.'[1] Readers interested in the case for the revised text should consult Lyon's notes to his edition, and the relevant chapter of Philip Horne's *Henry James and Revision*. Here I will present some more evidence to support my preference for the original text. I would emphasize that I am an admirer of Henry James's later style in his later fiction, but I think he made a mistake in trying to rework, in or around 1909, a story written thirty years previously, especially as the original was in its own way almost perfect.

Let us return to the first scene, which I discussed in the Introduction, at the point where Daisy asks Randolph where he got his pole (7): '"I bought it!" responded Randolph'. The New York Edition (NYE) has 'Randolph shouted'. It's a trivial change, but makes Randolph seem ruder and less 'smart' – to me, a loss of subtlety.

'You don't mean to say you're going to take it to Italy.'
'Yes, I am going to take it to Italy!' the child declared.

The NYE has: '"Yes, I'm going to take it t'Italy!" the child rang out.' The contraction 'I'm' in the revised text perhaps sounds more natural (though 'I am' could be Randolph's way of asserting his independence), but the contraction 't'Italy' is less convincing. In later life Henry James became increasingly disturbed by the slovenliness of American demotic speech – a concern he explicitly voiced in a 1905 lecture called 'The Question of Our Speech' – and one can't help suspecting that this affected his revision of the dialogue in 'Daisy Miller'. The NYE, for instance, has Daisy saying of Randolph, a little later in this scene, 'He don't like Europe' instead of the 1879 text's 'He doesn't like Europe' (10). One would trust Henry James's ear for how a young girl like Daisy would speak in the mid-1870s in the earlier text rather than the later. (An early American reviewer said he 'had succeeded to admiration in the difficult task of representing the manner in which such people as Mrs. and Miss Miller talk.')[2] As for the metaphorical 'rang out', it belongs to a whole series of elegant variations in the NYE on the basic speech-tags of the original story which make the prose more 'poetic' – the category in which James sought to place the story in his Preface. There are further examples of this process in the reworking of this passage:

> The young girl glanced over the front of her dress, and smoothed out a knot or two of ribbon. Then she rested her eyes upon the prospect again. 'Well, I guess you had better leave it somewhere,' she said, after a moment. (7)

The NYE has 'gave her sweet eyes to the prospect', which seems too fondly sentimental at this early stage of Winterbourne's acquaintance with the girl and loses the sense of Daisy's completely relaxed manner; and it has 'she dropped' instead of 'she said'. A few lines later there is an unfortunate repetition of 'drop' in the NYE when ' "Are you – a – going over the Simplon?" Winterbourne pursued, a little embarrassed' (7) becomes: ' "And are you – a – thinking of the Simplon?" he pursued with a slight drop of assurance.' It is unfortunate because obviously unintended: when elegant variation is the rule, then unmotivated repetition becomes intrusive. James may have looked for an alternative to 'a little embarrassed' because the word 'embarrassed' occurs twice not long afterwards in the original text – although *there* the repetition *is* motivated:

> ... Winterbourne presently risked an observation upon the beauty of the view. He was ceasing to be embarrassed, for he had begun to perceive that she was not in the least embarrassed herself. There had not been the slightest alteration in her charming complexion; she was evidently neither offended nor fluttered. If she looked another way when he spoke to her, and seemed not

particularly to hear him, this was simply her habit, her manner. Yet, as he talked a little more, and pointed out some of the objects of interest in the view, with which she appeared quite unacquainted, she gradually gave him more of the benefit of her glance; and then he saw that this glance was perfectly direct and unshrinking. It was not, however, what would have been called an immodest glance, for the young girl's eyes were singularly honest and fresh. They were wonderfully pretty eyes; and, indeed, Winterbourne had not for a long time seen anything prettier than his fair countrywoman's various features – her complexion, her nose, her ears, her teeth. (8)

This passage is much revised and expanded in the NYE:

Winterbourne presently risked an observation on the beauty of the view. He was ceasing to be in doubt, for he had begun to perceive that she was really not in the least embarrassed. She might be cold, she might be austere, she might even be prim, for that was apparently – he had already so generalized – what the most 'distant' American girls did: they came and planted themselves straight in front of you to show how rigidly unapproachable they were. There hadn't been the slightest flush in her fresh fairness however; so that she was clearly neither offended nor fluttered. Only she was composed – he had seen that before too – of charming little parts that didn't match and made no *ensemble*; and if she looked another way when he spoke to her, and seemed not particularly to hear him, this was simply her habit, her manner, the result of her having no idea whatever of 'form' (with such a tell-tale appendage as Randolph where in the world would she have got it?) in any such connexion. As he talked a little more and pointed out some of the objects of interest in the view, with which she seemed wholly unacquainted, she gradually, none the less, gave him more of the benefit of her attention; and then he saw that act unqualified by the faintest shadow of reserve. It wasn't however what would have been called a 'bold' front that she presented, for her expression was as decently limpid as the very cleanest water. Her eyes were the very prettiest conceivable, and indeed Winterbourne hadn't for a long

time seen anything prettier than his fair countrywoman's various
features – her complexion, her nose, her ears, her teeth.

There is more information in the second version – but is it really
needed, and is it all quite consistent? James is trying to render
Winterbourne's thought processes in the kind of finely discrim-
inated detail that is characteristic of his later fiction and at the
same time to hint at the fallibility of his hero's judgment. So he
tells us things which we can readily infer from the shorter
first version – for instance, that Randolph's behaviour is for
Winterbourne an index of the kind of manners Daisy is used to
– and he attributes to his hero a suspicion that she might be a
'cold . . . austere . . . prim' kind of girl deliberately defying his
male interest, which nothing in her demeanour has in fact
plausibly suggested. The NYE version is ruminative and diffuse, slowed and complicated by its more intricate syntax and
illustrative metaphors – 'little parts that didn't match and made
no ensemble . . . unqualified by the faintest shadow of reserve
. . . limpid as the very cleanest water' – compared to the 1879
version, which communicates the social dynamics of the situation more simply and more effectively: Winterbourne was
embarrassed, but now he is not embarrassed, because he per-
ceives Daisy is not embarrassed, and in the circumstances this
makes her a very unusual as well as a very pretty young woman.
The repetition of the word 'embarrassed' in this part of the
1879 text, which James reduced to just one occurrence in the
NYE, was entirely functional.

Admittedly, a few of James's revisions were genuine improve-
ments. When, for instance, Daisy tells him she is engaged and
immediately adds, 'You don't believe it!' (58) the 1879 text
has: 'He was silent a moment; and then, "Yes, I believe it!" he
said.' The NYE has: 'He asked himself, and it was for a moment
like testing a heart-beat; after which, "Yes, I believe it!" he
said.' The simile is very effective, partly because the word 'heart'
is closely associated with the emotion of love as well as with
life. But some of the revisions make one wonder what James
thought he had gained by them. In their penultimate meeting,
when Winterbourne is trying to convey to Daisy the disapproval

of Mrs Walker's circle, he asks her if she has not noticed anything, and she replies, in the 1879 text: 'I have noticed you. But I noticed you were as stiff as an umbrella the first time I saw you' (57). This homely simile is vivid and (like 'heart-beat') it has a contextual appropriateness: Winterbourne is just the kind of man, prudent and correctly dressed, to carry with him a tightly furled umbrella – and it is a *furled* umbrella that is evoked by 'stiff'. The epithet is one Daisy often applies perjoratively to Winterbourne in the course of the story. (When he tells her in the Pincio that she should get into Mrs Walker's carriage, she says, 'I never heard anything so stiff!' (44) and when on another occasion he says he can't dance, she says, 'Of course you don't dance; you're too stiff' (49).) In the NYE this speech becomes: 'But I noticed you've no more "give" than a ramrod the first time ever I saw you.' 'Ramrod' has military associations, which make this an unlikely figure of speech for Daisy to use, and inappropriate to describe Winterbourne; and the echo of Daisy's previous complaints about Winterbourne's 'stiffness' is lost.

There is a danger, when a writer revises his work after a very long interval, of disturbing, for the sake of a local effect, delicate relationships of sameness and difference between the component parts of the text that, even with an artist as self-conscious as Henry James, evolved organically and intuitively in the original creative process. One final example. At the end of the story, when Winterbourne reproaches Giovanelli for having taken Daisy to the Colosseum, he replies, 'For myself, I had no fear; and she wanted to go' (63). In the NYE he says: 'For myself I had no fear; and *she* – she did what she liked.' One might speculate that James thought that the phrase 'she did what she liked' sounded more like an epitaph on Daisy Miller's life than 'she wanted to go' and he set it up accordingly with Giovanelli's somewhat histrionic '*she*—she'. But for the attentive reader – and surely for Winterbourne – the phrase 'she wanted to go' evokes poignant echoes of the hero's and heroine's first two meetings by the lakeside at Vevey, scenes in which the verb 'to go' is constantly in use, as the question is debated and pondered whether Daisy will go to Chillon, and how, and with whom. One can't help thinking that in revising 'Daisy Miller' James neglected the wisdom of the popular American proverb 'If it ain't broke, don't fix it.'

The following elements of house style have been imposed on the text: '-ize' spellings rather than '-ise' in words like 'vocalizing'; single quotes instead of double (with double quotes then used for quotes within quotes). Closing punctuation in quotes has been standardized to match modern usage. Punctuation following italic words has been put into roman. On a couple of occasions erroneous question marks have been corrected.

D.L.

NOTES

1. John Lyon, ed., *Henry James: Selected Tales* (Harmondsworth: Penguin, 2001) p. xxxii.
2. Graham Clarke, ed., *Henry James: Critical Assessments: 1: Memories, Views and Writers* (Mountfield: Helm Information, 1991), p. 81.

Daisy Miller

A Study

I

At the little town of Vevey,[1] in Switzerland, there is a particularly comfortable hotel. There are, indeed, many hotels; for the entertainment of tourists is the business of the place, which, as many travellers will remember, is seated upon the edge of a remarkably blue lake – a lake that it behoves every tourist to visit. The shore of the lake presents an unbroken array of establishments of this order, of every category, from the 'grand hotel' of the newest fashion, with a chalk-white front, a hundred balconies, and a dozen flags flying from its roof, to the little Swiss *pension* of an elder day, with its name inscribed in German-looking lettering upon a pink or yellow wall, and an awkward summer-house in the angle of the garden. One of the hotels at Vevey, however, is famous, even classical, being distinguished from many of its upstart neighbours by an air both of luxury and of maturity. In this region, in the month of June, American travellers are extremely numerous; it may be said, indeed, that Vevey assumes at this period some of the characteristics of an American watering-place. There are sights and sounds which evoke a vision, an echo, of Newport and Saratoga.[2] There is a flitting hither and thither of 'stylish' young girls, a rustling of muslin flounces, a rattle of dance-music in the morning hours, a sound of high-pitched voices at all times. You receive an impression of these things at the excellent inn of the 'Trois Couronnes',[3] and are transported in fancy to the Ocean House or to Congress Hall.[4] But at the 'Trois Couronnes', it must be added, there are other features that are much at variance with these suggestions: neat German waiters, who look like secretaries of legation; Russian princesses sitting in the

garden; little Polish boys walking about, held by the hand, with
their governors; a view of the snowy crest of the Dent du Midi
and the picturesque towers of the Castle of Chillon.[5]

I hardly know whether it was the analogies or the differences
that were uppermost in the mind of a young American,
who, two or three years ago, sat in the garden of the 'Trois
Couronnes', looking about him, rather idly, at some of the
graceful objects I have mentioned. It was a beautiful summer
morning, and in whatever fashion the young American looked
at things, they must have seemed to him charming. He had
come from Geneva[6] the day before, by the little steamer, to see
his aunt, who was staying at the hotel – Geneva having been
for a long time his place of residence. But his aunt had a
headache – his aunt had almost always a headache – and now
she was shut up in her room, smelling camphor, so that he was
at liberty to wander about. He was some seven-and-twenty
years of age; when his friends spoke of him, they usually said
that he was at Geneva, 'studying'. When his enemies spoke of
him they said – but, after all, he had no enemies; he was an
extremely amiable fellow, and universally liked. What I should
say is, simply, that when certain persons spoke of him they
affirmed that the reason of his spending so much time at Geneva
was that he was extremely devoted to a lady who lived there –
a foreign lady – a person older than himself. Very few Americans – indeed I think none – had ever seen this lady, about
whom there were some singular stories. But Winterbourne
had an old attachment for the little metropolis of Calvinism;[7]
he had been put to school there as a boy, and he had afterwards gone to college there – circumstances which had led
to his forming a great many youthful friendships. Many of these
he had kept, and they were a source of great satisfaction
to him.

After knocking at his aunt's door and learning that she was
indisposed, he had taken a walk about the town, and then he
had come in to his breakfast. He had now finished his breakfast;
but he was drinking a small cup of coffee, which had been
served to him on a little table in the garden by one of the waiters
who looked like an *attaché*. At last he finished his coffee and

lit a cigarette. Presently a small boy came walking along the path – an urchin of nine or ten. The child, who was diminutive for his years, had an aged expression of countenance, a pale complexion, and sharp little features. He was dressed in knickerbockers, with red stockings, which displayed his poor little spindleshanks; he also wore a brilliant red cravat. He carried in his hand a long alpenstock, the sharp point of which he thrust into everything that he approached – the flower-beds, the garden-benches, the trains of the ladies' dresses. In front of Winterbourne he paused, looking at him with a pair of bright, penetrating little eyes.

'Will you give me a lump of sugar?' he asked, in a sharp, hard little voice – a voice immature, and yet, somehow, not young.

Winterbourne glanced at the small table near him, on which his coffee-service rested, and saw that several morsels of sugar remained. 'Yes, you may take one,' he answered; 'but I don't think sugar is good for little boys.'

This little boy stepped forward and carefully selected three of the coveted fragments, two of which he buried in the pocket of his knickerbockers, depositing the other as promptly in another place. He poked his alpenstock, lance-fashion, into Winterbourne's bench, and tried to crack the lump of sugar with his teeth.

'Oh, blazes; it's har-r-d!' he exclaimed, pronouncing the adjective in a peculiar manner.

Winterbourne had immediately perceived that he might have the honour of claiming him as a fellow-countryman. 'Take care you don't hurt your teeth,' he said, paternally.

'I haven't got any teeth to hurt. They have all come out. I have only got seven teeth. My mother counted them last night, and one came out right afterwards. She said she'd slap me if any more came out. I can't help it. It's this old Europe. It's the climate that makes them come out. In America they didn't come out. It's these hotels.'

Winterbourne was much amused. 'If you eat three lumps of sugar, your mother will certainly slap you,' he said.

'She's got to give me some candy, then,' rejoined his young

interlocutor. 'I can't get any candy here – any American candy. American candy's the best candy.'

'And are American little boys the best little boys?' asked Winterbourne.

'I don't know. I'm an American boy,' said the child.

'I see you are one of the best!' laughed Winterbourne.

'Are you an American man?' pursued this vivacious infant. And then, on Winterbourne's affirmative reply – 'American men are the best,' he declared.

His companion thanked him for the compliment; and the child, who had now got astride of his alpenstock, stood looking about him, while he attacked a second lump of sugar. Winterbourne wondered if he himself had been like this in his infancy, for he had been brought to Europe at about this age.

'Here comes my sister!' cried the child, in a moment. 'She's an American girl.'

Winterbourne looked along the path and saw a beautiful young lady advancing. 'American girls are the best girls,' he said, cheerfully, to his young companion.

'My sister ain't the best!' the child declared. 'She's always blowing at me.'

'I imagine that is your fault, not hers,' said Winterbourne. The young lady meanwhile had drawn near. She was dressed in white muslin, with a hundred frills and flounces, and knots of pale-coloured ribbon. She was bare-headed; but she balanced in her hand a large parasol, with a deep border of embroidery; and she was strikingly, admirably pretty. 'How pretty they are!' thought Winterbourne, straightening himself in his seat, as if he were prepared to rise.

The young lady paused in front of his bench, near the parapet of the garden, which overlooked the lake. The little boy had now converted his alpenstock into a vaulting-pole, by the aid of which he was springing about in the gravel, and kicking it up not a little.

'Randolph,' said the young lady, 'what *are* you doing?'

'I'm going up the Alps,' replied Randolph. 'This is the way!' And he gave another little jump, scattering the pebbles about Winterbourne's ears.

'That's the way they come down,' said Winterbourne.

'He's an American man!' cried Randolph, in his little hard voice.

The young lady gave no heed to this announcement, but looked straight at her brother. 'Well, I guess you had better be quiet,' she simply observed.

It seemed to Winterbourne that he had been in a manner presented. He got up and stepped slowly towards the young girl, throwing away his cigarette. 'This little boy and I have made acquaintance,' he said, with great civility. In Geneva, as he had been perfectly aware, a young man was not at liberty to speak to a young unmarried lady except under certain rarely-occurring conditions; but here at Vevey, what conditions could be better than these? – a pretty American girl coming and standing in front of you in a garden. This pretty American girl, however, on hearing Winterbourne's observation, simply glanced at him; she then turned her head and looked over the parapet, at the lake and the opposite mountains. He wondered whether he had gone too far; but he decided that he must advance farther, rather than retreat. While he was thinking of something else to say, the young lady turned to the little boy again.

'I should like to know where you got that pole,' she said.

'I bought it!' responded Randolph.

'You don't mean to say you're going to take it to Italy.'

'Yes, I am going to take it to Italy!' the child declared.

The young girl glanced over the front of her dress, and smoothed out a knot or two of ribbon. Then she rested her eyes upon the prospect again. 'Well, I guess you had better leave it somewhere,' she said, after a moment.

'Are you going to Italy?' Winterbourne inquired, in a tone of great respect.

The young lady glanced at him again. 'Yes, sir,' she replied. And she said nothing more.

'Are you – a – going over the Simplon?'[8] Winterbourne pursued, a little embarrassed.

'I don't know,' she said. 'I suppose it's some mountain. Randolph, what mountain are we going over?'

'Going where?' the child demanded.

'To Italy,' Winterbourne explained.

'I don't know,' said Randolph. 'I don't want to go to Italy. I want to go to America.'

'Oh, Italy is a beautiful place!' rejoined the young man.

'Can you get candy there?' Randolph loudly inquired.

'I hope not,' said his sister. 'I guess you have had enough candy, and mother thinks so too.'

'I haven't had any for ever so long – for a hundred weeks!' cried the boy, still jumping about.

The young lady inspected her flounces and smoothed her ribbons again; and Winterbourne presently risked an observation upon the beauty of the view. He was ceasing to be embarrassed, for he had begun to perceive that she was not in the least embarrassed herself. There had not been the slightest alteration in her charming complexion; she was evidently neither offended nor fluttered. If she looked another way when he spoke to her, and seemed not particularly to hear him, this was simply her habit, her manner. Yet, as he talked a little more, and pointed out some of the objects of interest in the view, with which she appeared quite unacquainted, she gradually gave him more of the benefit of her glance; and then he saw that this glance was perfectly direct and unshrinking. It was not, however, what would have been called an immodest glance, for the young girl's eyes were singularly honest and fresh. They were wonderfully pretty eyes; and, indeed, Winterbourne had not seen for a long time anything prettier than his fair countrywoman's various features – her complexion, her nose, her ears, her teeth. He had a great relish for feminine beauty; he was addicted to observing and analysing it; and as regards this young lady's face he made several observations. It was not at all insipid, but it was not exactly expressive; and though it was eminently delicate Winterbourne mentally accused it – very forgivingly – of a want of finish. He thought it very possible that Master Randolph's sister was a coquette; he was sure she had a spirit of her own; but in her bright, sweet, superficial little visage there was no mockery, no irony. Before long it became obvious that she was much disposed towards conversation. She told him that they were going to Rome for the winter – she and her mother and Randolph. She asked him if he was a 'real American'; she wouldn't have taken him for one; he seemed more like a German – this was said after a little hesitation, especially when he spoke. Winterbourne, laughing, answered that he had met Germans who spoke like Americans; but that he had not, so far as he remembered, met an American who spoke like a German. Then he asked her if she would not be more comfortable in sitting upon the bench which he had just quitted. She answered that she liked standing up and walking about; but she presently sat down. She told him she was from New York State – 'if you know where that is'. Winterbourne learned more about her by catching hold of her small, slippery brother and making him stand a few minutes by his side.

'Tell me your name, my boy,' he said.

'Randolph C. Miller,' said the boy, sharply. 'And I'll tell you her name;' and he levelled his alpenstock at his sister.

'You had better wait till you are asked!' said this young lady, calmly.

'I should like very much to know your name,' said Winterbourne.

'Her name is Daisy Miller!' cried the child. 'But that isn't her real name; that isn't her name on her cards.'

'It's a pity you haven't got one of my cards!' said Miss Miller.

'Her real name is Annie P. Miller,' the boy went on.

'Ask him *his* name,' said his sister, indicating Winterbourne.

But on this point Randolph seemed perfectly indifferent; he continued to supply information with regard to his own family. 'My father's name is Ezra B. Miller,' he announced. 'My father ain't in Europe; my father's in a better place than Europe.'

Winterbourne imagined for a moment that this was the manner in which the child had been taught to intimate that Mr. Miller had been removed to the sphere of celestial rewards. But Randolph immediately added, 'My father's in Schenectady. He's got a big business. My father's rich, you bet.'

'Well!' ejaculated Miss Miller, lowering her parasol and looking at the embroidered border. Winterbourne presently released

the child, who departed, dragging his alpenstock along the
path. 'He doesn't like Europe,' said the young girl. 'He wants
to go back.'

'To Schenectady, you mean?'

'Yes; he wants to go right home. He hasn't got any boys here.
There is one boy here, but he always goes round with a teacher;
they won't let him play.'

'And your brother hasn't any teacher?' Winterbourne
inquired.

'Mother thought of getting him one, to travel round with us.
There was a lady told her of a very good teacher; an American
lady – perhaps you know her – Mrs. Sanders. I think she came
from Boston. She told her of this teacher, and we thought of
getting him to travel round with us. But Randolph said he didn't
want a teacher travelling round with us. He said he wouldn't
have lessons when he was in the cars.[10] And we *are* in the cars
about half the time. There was an English lady we met in the
cars – I think her name was Miss Featherstone; perhaps you
know her. She wanted to know why I didn't give Randolph
lessons – give him "instruction", she called it. I guess he could
give me more instruction than I could give him. He's very smart.'

'Yes,' said Winterbourne; 'he seems very smart.'

'Mother's going to get a teacher for him as soon as we get to
Italy. Can you get good teachers in Italy?'

'Very good, I should think,' said Winterbourne.

'Or else she's going to find some school. He ought to learn
some more. He's only nine. He's going to college.' And in this
way Miss Miller continued to converse upon the affairs of her
family, and upon other topics. She sat there with her extremely
pretty hands, ornamented with very brilliant rings, folded in
her lap, and with her pretty eyes now resting upon those of
Winterbourne, now wandering over the garden, the people who
passed by, and the beautiful view. She talked to Winterbourne
as if she had known him a long time. He found it very pleasant.
It was many years since he had heard a young girl talk so much.
It might have been said of this unknown young lady, who had
come and sat down beside him upon a bench, that she chattered.
She was very quiet, she sat in a charming tranquil attitude; but

her lips and her eyes were constantly moving. She had a soft, slender, agreeable voice, and her tone was decidedly sociable. She gave Winterbourne a history of her movements and intentions, and those of her mother and brother, in Europe, and enumerated, in particular, the various hotels at which they had stopped. 'That English lady in the cars,' she said – 'Miss Featherstone – asked me if we didn't all live in hotels in America. I told her I had never been in so many hotels in my life as since I came to Europe. I have never seen so many – it's nothing but hotels.' But Miss Miller did not make this remark with a querulous accent; she appeared to be in the best humour with everything. She declared that the hotels were very good, when once you got used to their ways, and that Europe was perfectly sweet. She was not disappointed – not a bit. Perhaps it was because she had heard so much about it before. She had ever so many intimate friends that had been there ever so many times. And then she had had ever so many dresses and things from Paris. Whenever she put on a Paris dress she felt as if she were in Europe.

'It was a kind of a wishing-cap,' said Winterbourne.

'Yes,' said Miss Miller, without examining this analogy; 'it always made me wish I was here. But I needn't have done that for dresses. I am sure they send all the pretty ones to America; you see the most frightful things here. The only thing I don't like,' she proceeded, 'is the society. There isn't any society; or, if there is, I don't know where it keeps itself. Do you? I suppose there is some society somewhere, but I haven't seen anything of it. I'm very fond of society, and I have always had a great deal of it. I don't mean only in Schenectady, but in New York. I used to go to New York every winter. In New York I had lots of society. Last winter I had seventeen dinners given me; and three of them were by gentlemen,' added Daisy Miller. 'I have more friends in New York than in Schenectady – more gentlemen friends; and more young lady friends too,' she resumed in a moment. She paused again for an instant; she was looking at Winterbourne with all her prettiness in her lively eyes and in her light, slightly monotonous smile. 'I have always had,' she said, 'a great deal of gentlemen's society.'

Poor Winterbourne was amused, perplexed, and decidedly charmed. He had never yet heard a young girl express herself in just this fashion; never, at least, save in cases where to say such things seemed a kind of demonstrative evidence of a certain laxity of deportment. And yet was he to accuse Miss Daisy Miller of actual or potential *inconduite*,[11] as they said at Geneva? He felt that he had lived at Geneva so long that he had lost a good deal; he had become dishabituated to the American tone. Never, indeed, since he had grown old enough to appreciate things, had he encountered a young American girl of so pronounced a type as this. Certainly she was very charming; but how deucedly sociable! Was she simply a pretty girl from New York State – were they all like that, the pretty girls who had a good deal of gentlemen's society? Or was she also a designing, an audacious, an unscrupulous young person? Winterbourne had lost his instinct in this matter, and his reason could not help him. Miss Daisy Miller looked extremely innocent. Some people had told him that, after all, American girls were exceedingly innocent; and others had told him that, after all, they were not. He was inclined to think Miss Daisy Miller was a flirt – a pretty American flirt. He had never, as yet, had any relations with young ladies of this category. He had known, here in Europe, two or three women – persons older than Miss Daisy Miller, and provided, for respectability's sake, with husbands – who were great coquettes – dangerous, terrible women, with whom one's relations were liable to take a serious turn. But this young girl was not a coquette in that sense; she was very unsophisticated; she was only a pretty American flirt. Winterbourne was almost grateful for having found the formula that applied to Miss Daisy Miller. He leaned back in his seat; he remarked to himself that she had the most charming nose he had ever seen; he wondered what were the regular conditions and limitations of one's intercourse with a pretty American flirt. It presently became apparent that he was on the way to learn.

'Have you been to that old castle?' asked the young girl, pointing with her parasol to the far-gleaming walls of the Château de Chillon.

'Yes, formerly, more than once,' said Winterbourne. 'You too, I suppose, have seen it?'

'No; we haven't been there. I want to go there dreadfully. Of course I mean to go there. I wouldn't go away from here without having seen that old castle.'

'It's a very pretty excursion,' said Winterbourne, 'and very easy to make. You can drive, you know, or you can go by the little steamer.'

'You can go in the cars,' said Miss Miller.

'Yes; you can go in the cars,' Winterbourne assented.

'Our courier says they take you right up to the castle,' the young girl continued. 'We were going last week; but my mother gave out. She suffers dreadfully from dyspepsia. She said she couldn't go. Randolph wouldn't go either; he says he doesn't think much of old castles. But I guess we'll go this week, if we can get Randolph.'

'Your brother is not interested in ancient monuments?' Winterbourne inquired, smiling.

'He says he don't care much about old castles. He's only nine. He wants to stay at the hotel. Mother's afraid to leave him alone, and the courier won't stay with him; so we haven't been to many places. But it will be too bad if we don't go up there.' And Miss Miller pointed again at the Château de Chillon.

'I should think it might be arranged,' said Winterbourne. 'Couldn't you get some one to stay – for the afternoon – with Randolph?'

Miss Miller looked at him a moment; and then, very placidly – 'I wish *you* would stay with him!' she said.

Winterbourne hesitated a moment. 'I would much rather go to Chillon with you.'

'With me?' asked the young girl, with the same placidity.

She didn't rise, blushing, as a young girl at Geneva would have done; and yet Winterbourne, conscious that he had been very bold, thought it possible she was offended. 'With your mother,' he answered very respectfully.

But it seemed that both his audacity and his respect were lost upon Miss Daisy Miller. 'I guess my mother won't go, after all,' she said. 'She don't like to ride round in the afternoon. But did you really mean what you said just now; that you would like to go up there?'

'Most earnestly,' Winterbourne declared.

'Then we may arrange it. If mother will stay with Randolph, I guess Eugenio will.'

'Eugenio?' the young man inquired.

'Eugenio's our courier. He doesn't like to stay with Randolph; he's the most fastidious man I ever saw. But he's a splendid courier. I guess he'll stay at home with Randolph if mother does, and then we can go to the castle.'

Winterbourne reflected for an instant as lucidly as possible – 'we' could only mean Miss Daisy Miller and himself. This programme seemed almost too agreeable for credence; he felt as if he ought to kiss the young lady's hand. Possibly he would have done so – and quite spoiled the project; but at this moment another person – presumably Eugenio – appeared. A tall, handsome man, with superb whiskers, wearing a velvet morning-coat and a brilliant watch-chain, approached Miss Miller, looking sharply at her companion. 'Oh, Eugenio!' said Miss Miller, with the friendliest accent.

Eugenio had looked at Winterbourne from head to foot; he now bowed gravely to the young lady. 'I have the honour to inform mademoiselle that luncheon is upon the table.'

Miss Miller slowly rose. 'See here, Eugenio,' she said. 'I'm going to that old castle, any way.'

'To the Château de Chillon, mademoiselle?' the courier inquired. 'Mademoiselle has made arrangements?' he added, in a tone which struck Winterbourne as very impertinent.

Eugenio's tone apparently threw, even to Miss Miller's own apprehension, a slightly ironical light upon the young girl's situation. She turned to Winterbourne, blushing a little – a very little. 'You won't back out?' she said.

'I shall not be happy till we go!' he protested.

'And you are staying in this hotel?' she went on. 'And you are really an American?'

The courier stood looking at Winterbourne, offensively. The young man, at least, thought his manner of looking an offence to Miss Miller; it conveyed an imputation that she 'picked up' acquaintances. 'I shall have the honour of presenting to you a person who will tell you all about me,' he said smiling, and referring to his aunt.

'Oh, well, we'll go some day,' said Miss Miller. And she gave him a smile and turned away. She put up her parasol and walked back to the inn beside Eugenio. Winterbourne stood looking after her; and as she moved away, drawing her muslin furbelows over the gravel, said to himself that she had the *tournure*[12] of a princess.

II

He had, however, engaged to do more than proved feasible, in promising to present his aunt, Mrs. Costello, to Miss Daisy Miller. As soon as the former lady had got better of her headache he waited upon her in her apartment; and, after the proper inquiries in regard to her health, he asked her if she had observed, in the hotel, an American family – a mamma, a daughter, and a little boy.

'And a courier?' said Mrs. Costello. 'Oh, yes, I have observed them. Seen them – heard them – and kept out of their way.' Mrs. Costello was a widow with a fortune; a person of much distinction, who frequently intimated that, if she were not so dreadfully liable to sick-headaches, she would probably have left a deeper impress upon her time. She had a long pale face, a high nose, and a great deal of very striking white hair, which she wore in large puffs and *rouleaux*[1] over the top of her head. She had two sons married in New York, and another who was now in Europe. This young man was amusing himself at Homburg,[2] and, though he was on his travels, was rarely perceived to visit any particular city at the moment selected by his mother for her own appearance there. Her nephew, who had come up to Vevey expressly to see her, was therefore more attentive than those who, as she said, were nearer to her. He had imbibed at Geneva the idea that one must always be attentive to one's aunt. Mrs. Costello had not seen him for many years, and she was greatly pleased with him, manifesting her approbation by initiating him into many of the secrets of that social sway which, as she gave him to understand, she exerted in the American capital. She admitted that she was very exclusive; but, if he were acquainted with New York, he would see that one had to be. And her picture of the minutely hierarchical constitution of the society of that city, which she presented to him in many different lights, was, to Winterbourne's imagination, almost oppressively striking.

He immediately perceived, from her tone, that Miss Daisy Miller's place in the social scale was low. 'I am afraid you don't approve of them,' he said.

'They are very common,' Mrs. Costello declared. 'They are the sort of Americans that one does one's duty by not – not accepting.'

'Ah, you don't accept them?' said the young man.

'I can't, my dear Frederick. I would if I could, but I can't.'

'The young girl is very pretty,' said Winterbourne, in a moment.

'Of course she's pretty. But she is very common.'

'I see what you mean, of course,' said Winterbourne, after another pause.

'She has that charming look that they all have,' his aunt resumed. 'I can't think where they pick it up; and she dresses in perfection – no, you don't know how well she dresses. I can't think where they get their taste.'

'But, my dear aunt, she is not, after all, a Comanche savage.'

'She is a young lady,' said Mrs. Costello, 'who has an intimacy with her mamma's courier!'

'An intimacy with the courier?' the young man demanded.

'Oh, the mother is just as bad! They treat the courier like a familiar friend – like a gentleman. I shouldn't wonder if he dines with them. Very likely they have never seen a man with such good manners, such fine clothes, so like a gentleman. He probably corresponds to the young lady's idea of a Count. He sits with them in the garden, in the evening. I think he smokes.'

Winterbourne listened with interest to these disclosures; they helped him to make up his mind about Miss Daisy. Evidently she was rather wild. 'Well,' he said, 'I am not a courier, and yet she was very charming to me.'

'You had better have said at first,' said Mrs. Costello with dignity, 'that you had made her acquaintance.'

'We simply met in the garden, and we talked a bit.'

'*Tout bonnement!*[3] And pray what did you say?'

'I said I should take the liberty of introducing her to my admirable aunt.'

'I am much obliged to you.'

'It was to guarantee my respectability,' said Winterbourne.

'And pray who is to guarantee hers?'

'Ah, you are cruel!' said the young man. 'She's a very nice girl.'

'You don't say that as if you believed it,' Mrs. Costello observed.

'She is completely uncultivated,' Winterbourne went on. 'But she is wonderfully pretty, and, in short, she is very nice. To prove that I believe it, I am going to take her to the Château de Chillon.'

'You two are going off there together? I should say it proved just the contrary. How long had you known her, may I ask, when this interesting project was formed? You haven't been twenty-four hours in the house.'

'I had known her half-an-hour!' said Winterbourne, smiling.

'Dear me!' cried Mrs. Costello. 'What a dreadful girl!'

Her nephew was silent for some moments. 'You really think, then,' he began, earnestly, and with a desire for trustworthy information – 'you really think that –' But he paused again.

'Think what, sir?' said his aunt.

'That she is the sort of young lady who expects a man – sooner or later – to carry her off?'

'I haven't the least idea what such young ladies expect a man to do. But I really think that you had better not meddle with little American girls that are uncultivated, as you call them. You have lived too long out of the country. You will be sure to make some great mistake. You are too innocent.'

'My dear aunt, I am not so innocent,' said Winterbourne, smiling and curling his moustache.

'You are too guilty, then!'

Winterbourne continued to curl his moustache, meditatively. 'You won't let the poor girl know you then?' he asked at last.

'Is it literally true that she is going to the Château de Chillon with you?'

'I think that she fully intends it.'

'Then, my dear Frederick,' said Mrs. Costello, 'I must decline the honour of her acquaintance. I am an old woman, but I am not too old – thank Heaven – to be shocked!'

'But don't they all do these things – the young girls in America?' Winterbourne inquired.

Mrs. Costello stared a moment. 'I should like to see my granddaughters do them!' she declared, grimly.

This seemed to throw some light upon the matter, for Winterbourne remembered to have heard that his pretty cousins in New York were 'tremendous flirts'. If, therefore, Miss Daisy Miller exceeded the liberal license allowed to these young ladies, it was probable that anything might be expected of her. Winterbourne was impatient to see her again, and he was vexed with himself that, by instinct, he should not appreciate her justly.

Though he was impatient to see her, he hardly knew what he should say to her about his aunt's refusal to become acquainted with her; but he discovered, promptly enough, that with Miss Daisy Miller there was no great need of walking on tiptoe. He found her that evening in the garden, wandering about in the warm starlight, like an indolent sylph, and swinging to and fro the largest fan he had ever beheld. It was ten o'clock. He had dined with his aunt, had been sitting with her since dinner, and had just taken leave of her till the morrow. Miss Daisy Miller seemed very glad to see him; she declared it was the longest evening she had ever passed.

'Have you been all alone?' he asked.

'I have been walking round with mother. But mother gets tired walking round,' she answerd.

'Has she gone to bed?'

'No; she doesn't like to go to bed,' said the young girl. 'She doesn't sleep – not three hours. She says she doesn't know how she lives. She's dreadfully nervous. I guess she sleeps more than she thinks. She's gone somewhere after Randolph; she wants to try to get him to go to bed. He doesn't like to go to bed.'

'Let us hope she will persuade him,' observed Winterbourne.

'She will talk to him all she can; but he doesn't like her to talk to him,' said Miss Daisy, opening her fan. 'She's going to try to get Eugenio to talk to him. But he isn't afraid of Eugenio. Eugenio's a splendid courier, but he can't make much impression on Randolph! I don't believe he'll go to bed before eleven.' It appeared that Randolph's vigil was in fact triumphantly prolonged, for Winterbourne strolled about with the young girl for some time without meeting her mother. 'I have been looking round for that lady you want to introduce me to,' his companion resumed. 'She's your aunt.' Then, on Winterbourne's admitting the fact, and expressing some curiosity as to how she had learned it, she said she had heard all about Mrs. Costello from the chambermaid. She was very quiet and very *comme il faut*;[4] she wore white puffs; she spoke to no one, and she never dined at the *table d'hôte*.[5] Every two days she had a headache. 'I think that's a lovely description, headache and all!' said Miss Daisy, chattering along in her thin, gay voice. 'I want to know her ever so much. I know just what *your* aunt would be; I know I should like her. She would be very exclusive. I like a lady to be exclusive; I'm dying to be exclusive myself. Well, we *are* exclusive, mother and I. We don't speak to every one – or they don't speak to us. I suppose it's about the same thing. Any way, I shall be ever so glad to know your aunt.'

Winterbourne was embarrassed. 'She would be most happy,' he said; 'but I am afraid those headaches will interfere.'

The young girl looked at him through the dusk. 'But I suppose she doesn't have a headache every day,' she said, sympathetically.

Winterbourne was silent a moment. 'She tells me she does,' he answered at last – not knowing what to say.

Miss Daisy Miller stopped and stood looking at him. Her prettiness was still visible in the darkness; she was opening and closing her enormous fan. 'She doesn't want to know me!' she said, suddenly. 'Why don't you say so? You needn't be afraid. I'm not afraid!' And she gave a little laugh.

Winterbourne fancied there was a tremor in her voice; he was touched, shocked, mortified by it. 'My dear young lady,' he protested, 'she knows no one. It's her wretched health.'

The young girl walked on a few steps, laughing still. 'You needn't be afraid,' she repeated. 'Why should she want to know me?' Then she paused again; she was close to the parapet of the garden, and in front of her was the starlit lake. There was a vague sheen upon its surface, and in the distance were dimly-seen mountain forms. Daisy Miller looked out upon the mysterious prospect, and then she gave another little laugh. 'Gracious! she *is* exclusive!' she said. Winterbourne wondered whether she was seriously wounded, and for a moment almost wished that her sense of injury might be such as to make it becoming in him to attempt to reassure and comfort her. He had a pleasant sense that she would be very approachable for consolatory purposes. He felt then, for the instant, quite ready to sacrifice his aunt, conversationally; to admit that she was a proud, rude woman, and to declare that they needn't mind her. But before he had time to commit himself to this perilous mixture of gallantry and impiety, the young lady, resuming her walk, gave an exclamation in quite another tone. 'Well; here's mother! I guess she hasn't got Randolph to go to bed.' The figure of a lady appeared, at a distance, very indistinct in the darkness, and advancing with a slow and wavering movement. Suddenly it seemed to pause.

'Are you sure it is your mother? Can you distinguish her in this thick dusk?' Winterbourne asked.

'Well!' cried Miss Daisy Miller, with a laugh, 'I guess I know my own mother. And when she has got on my shawl, too! She is always wearing my things.'

The lady in question, ceasing to advance, hovered vaguely about the spot at which she had checked her steps.

'I am afraid your mother doesn't see you,' said Winterbourne. 'Or perhaps,' he added – thinking, with Miss Miller, the joke permissible – 'perhaps she feels guilty about your shawl.'

'Oh, it's a fearful old thing!' the young girl replied, serenely. 'I told her she could wear it. She won't come here, because she sees you.'

'Ah, then,' said Winterbourne, 'I had better leave you.'

'Oh no; come on!' urged Miss Daisy Miller.

'I'm afraid your mother doesn't approve of my walking with you.'

Miss Miller gave him a serious glance. 'It isn't for me; it's for you – that is, it's for *her*. Well; I don't know who it's for! But mother doesn't like any of my gentlemen friends. She's right down timid. She always makes a fuss if I introduce a gentleman. But I *do* introduce them – almost always. If I didn't introduce my gentlemen friends to mother,' the young girl added, in her little soft, flat monotone, 'I shouldn't think I was natural.'

'To introduce me,' said Winterbourne, 'you must know my name.' And he proceeded to pronounce it.

'Oh, dear; I can't say all that!' said his companion, with a laugh. But by this time they had come up to Mrs. Miller, who, as they drew near, walked to the parapet of the garden and leaned upon it, looking intently at the lake and turning her back upon them. 'Mother!' said the young girl, in a tone of decision. Upon this the elder lady turned round. 'Mr. Winterbourne,' said Miss Daisy Miller, introducing the young man very frankly and prettily. 'Common' she was, as Mrs. Costello had pronounced her; yet it was a wonder to Winterbourne that, with her commonness, she had a singularly delicate grace.

Her mother was a small, spare, light person, with a wandering eye, a very exiguous nose, and a large forehead, decorated with a certain amount of thin, much-frizzled hair. Like her daughter, Mrs. Miller was dressed with extreme elegance; she had enormous diamonds in her ears. So far as Winterbourne could observe, she gave him no greeting – she certainly was not looking at him. Daisy was near her, pulling her shawl straight. 'What are you doing, poking round here?' this young lady inquired; but by no means with that harshness of accent which her choice of words may imply.

'I don't know,' said her mother, turning towards the lake again.

'I shouldn't think you'd want that shawl!' Daisy exclaimed.

'Well – I do!' her mother answered, with a little laugh.

'Did you get Randolph to go to bed?' asked the young girl.

'No; I couldn't induce him,' said Mrs. Miller, very gently. 'He wants to talk to the waiter. He likes to talk to that waiter.'

'I was telling Mr. Winterbourne,' the young girl went on; and to the young man's ear her tone might have indicated that she had been uttering his name all her life.

'Oh, yes!' said Winterbourne; 'I have the pleasure of knowing your son.'

Randolph's mamma was silent; she turned her attention to the lake. But at last she spoke. 'Well, I don't see how he lives!'

'Anyhow, it isn't so bad as it was at Dover,' said Daisy Miller.

'And what occurred at Dover?' Winterbourne asked.

'He wouldn't go to bed at all. I guess he sat up all night – in the public parlour. He wasn't in bed at twelve o'clock: I know that.'

'It was half-past twelve,' declared Mrs. Miller, with mild emphasis.

'Does he sleep much during the day?' Winterbourne demanded.

'I guess he doesn't sleep much,' Daisy rejoined.

'I wish he would!' said her mother. 'It seems as if he couldn't.'

'I think he's real tiresome,' Daisy pursued.

Then, for some moments, there was silence. 'Well, Daisy Miller,' said the elder lady, presently, 'I shouldn't think you'd want to talk against your own brother!'

'Well, he *is* tiresome, mother,' said Daisy, quite without the asperity of a retort.

'He's only nine,' urged Mrs. Miller.

'Well, he wouldn't go to that castle,' said the young girl. 'I'm going there with Mr. Winterbourne.'

To this announcement, very placidly made, Daisy's mamma offered no response. Winterbourne took for granted that she deeply disapproved of the projected excursion; but he said to himself that she was a simple, easily-managed person, and that a few deferential protestations would take the edge from her displeasure. 'Yes,' he began; 'your daughter has kindly allowed me the honour of being her guide.'

Mrs. Miller's wandering eyes attached themselves, with a sort of appealing air, to Daisy, who, however, strolled a few steps farther, gently humming to herself. 'I presume you will go in the cars,' said her mother.

'Yes; or in the boat,' said Winterbourne.

'Well, of course, I don't know,' Mrs. Miller rejoined. 'I have never been to that castle.'

'It is a pity you shouldn't go,' said Winterbourne, beginning to feel reassured as to her opposition. And yet he was quite prepared to find that, as a matter of course, she meant to accompany her daughter.

'We've been thinking ever so much about going,' she pursued; 'but it seems as if we couldn't. Of course Daisy – she wants to go round. But there's a lady here – I don't know her name – she says she shouldn't think we'd want to go to see castles *here*; she should think we'd want to wait till we got to Italy. It seems as if there would be so many there,' continued Mrs. Miller, with an air of increasing confidence. 'Of course, we only want to see the principal ones. We visited several in England,' she presently added.

'Ah, yes! in England there are beautiful castles,' said Winterbourne. 'But Chillon, here, is very well worth seeing.'

'Well, if Daisy feels up to it –,' said Mrs. Miller, in a tone impregnated with a sense of the magnitude of the enterprise. 'It seems as if there was nothing she wouldn't undertake.'

'Oh, I think she'll enjoy it!' Winterbourne declared. And he desired more and more to make it a certainty that he was to have the privilege of a *tête-à-tête* with the young lady, who was still strolling along in front of them, softly vocalizing. 'You are not disposed, madam,' he inquired, 'to undertake it yourself?'

Daisy's mother looked at him, an instant, askance, and then walked forward in silence. Then – 'I guess she had better go alone,' she said, simply.

Winterbourne observed to himself that this was a very different type of maternity from that of the vigilant matrons who massed themselves in the forefront of social intercourse in the dark old city at the other end of the lake. But his meditations were interrupted by hearing his name very distinctly pronounced by Mrs. Miller's unprotected daughter.

'Mr. Winterbourne!' murmured Daisy.

'Mademoiselle!' said the young man.

'Don't you want to take me out in a boat?'

'At present?' he asked.

'Of course!' said Daisy.

'Well, Annie Miller!' exclaimed her mother.

'I beg you, madam, to let her go,' said Winterbourne, ardently; for he had never yet enjoyed the sensation of guiding through the summer starlight a skiff freighted with a fresh and beautiful young girl.

'I shouldn't think she'd want to,' said her mother. 'I should think she'd rather go indoors.'

'I'm sure Mr. Winterbourne wants to take me,' Daisy declared. 'He's so awfully devoted!'

'I will row you over to Chillon, in the starlight.'

'I don't believe it!' said Daisy.

'Well!' ejaculated the elder lady again.

'You haven't spoken to me for half-an-hour,' her daughter went on.

'I have been having some very pleasant conversation with your mother,' said Winterbourne.

'Well; I want you to take me out in a boat!' Daisy repeated. They had all stopped, and she had turned round and was looking at Winterbourne. Her face wore a charming smile, her pretty eyes were gleaming, she was swinging her great fan about. No; it's impossible to be prettier than that, thought Winterbourne.

'There are half-a-dozen boats moored at that landing-place,' he said, pointing to certain steps which descended from the garden to the lake. 'If you will do me the honour to accept my arm, we will go and select one of them.'

Daisy stood there smiling; she threw back her head and gave a little light laugh. 'I like a gentleman to be formal!' she declared.

'I assure you it's a formal offer.'

'I was bound I would make you say something,' Daisy went on.

'You see it's not very difficult,' said Winterbourne. 'But I am afraid you are chaffing me.'

'I think not, sir,' remarked Mrs. Miller, very gently.

'Do, then, let me give you a row,' he said to the young girl.

'It's quite lovely, the way you say that!' cried Daisy.

'It will be still more lovely to do it.'

'Yes, it would be lovely!' said Daisy. But she made no movement to accompany him; she only stood there laughing.

'I should think you had better find out what time it is,' interposed her mother.

'It is eleven o'clock, madam,' said a voice, with a foreign accent, out of the neighbouring darkness; and Winterbourne, turning, perceived the florid personage who was in attendance upon the two ladies. He had apparently just approached.

'Oh, Eugenio,' said Daisy, 'I am going out in a boat!'

Eugenio bowed. 'At eleven o'clock, mademoiselle?'

'I am going with Mr. Winterbourne. This very minute.'

'Do tell her she can't,' said Mrs. Miller to the courier.

'I think you had better not go out in a boat, mademoiselle,' Eugenio declared.

Winterbourne wished to Heaven this pretty girl were not so familiar with her courier; but he said nothing.

'I suppose you don't think it's proper!' Daisy exclaimed. 'Eugenio doesn't think anything's proper.'

'I am at your service,' said Winterbourne.

'Does mademoiselle propose to go alone?' asked Eugenio of Mrs. Miller.

'Oh, no; with this gentleman!' answered Daisy's mamma.

The courier looked for a moment at Winterbourne – the latter thought he was smiling – and then, solemnly, with a bow, 'As mademoiselle pleases!' he said.

'Oh, I hoped you would make a fuss!' said Daisy. 'I don't care to go now.'

'I myself shall make a fuss if you don't go,' said Winterbourne.

'That's all I want – a little fuss!' And the young girl began to laugh again.

'Mr. Randolph has gone to bed!' the courier announced, frigidly.

'Oh, Daisy; now we can go!' said Mrs. Miller.

Daisy turned away from Winterbourne, looking at him,

smiling and fanning herself. 'Good night,' she said; 'I hope you are disappointed, or disgusted, or something!'

He looked at her, taking the hand she offered him. 'I am puzzled,' he answered.

'Well; I hope it won't keep you awake!' she said, very smartly; and, under the escort of the privileged Eugenio, the two ladies passed towards the house.

Winterbourne stood looking after them; he was indeed puzzled. He lingered beside the lake for a quarter of an hour, turning over the mystery of the young girl's sudden familiarities and caprices. But the only very definite conclusion he came to was that he should enjoy deucedly 'going off' with her somewhere.

Two days afterwards he went off with her to the Castle of Chillon. He waited for her in the large hall of the hotel, where the couriers, the servants, the foreign tourists were lounging about and staring. It was not the place he would have chosen, but she had appointed it. She came tripping downstairs, buttoning her long gloves, squeezing her folded parasol against her pretty figure, dressed in the perfection of a soberly elegant travelling-costume. Winterbourne was a man of imagination and, as our ancestors used to say, of sensibility; as he looked at her dress and, on the great staircase, her little rapid, confiding step, he felt as if there were something romantic going forward. He could have believed he was going to elope with her. He passed out with her among all the idle people that were assembled there; they were all looking at her very hard; she had begun to chatter as soon as she joined him. Winterbourne's preference had been that they should be conveyed to Chillon in a carriage; but she expressed a lively wish to go in the little steamer; she declared that she had a passion for steamboats. There was always such a lovely breeze upon the water, and you saw such lots of people. The sail was not long, but Winterbourne's companion found time to say a great many things. To the young man himself their little excursion was so much of an escapade – an adventure – that, even allowing for her habitual sense of freedom, he had some expectation of seeing her regard it in the same way. But it must be confessed that, in this particular, he was disappointed. Daisy Miller was extremely animated, she was in charming spirits; but she was apparently not at all excited; she was not fluttered; she avoided neither his eyes nor those of any one else; she blushed neither when she looked at him nor when she saw that people were looking at her. People continued to look at her a great deal, and Winterbourne took much satisfaction in his pretty companion's distinguished air. He had been a little afraid that she would talk loud, laugh overmuch, and even, perhaps, desire to move about the boat a good deal. But he quite forgot his fears; he sat smiling, with his eyes upon her face, while, without moving from her place, she delivered herself of a great number of original reflections. It was the most charming garrulity he had ever heard. He had assented to the idea that she was 'common'; but was she so, after all, or was he simply getting used to her commonness? Her conversation was chiefly of what metaphysicians term the objective cast; but every now and then it took a subjective turn.

'What on *earth* are you so grave about?' she suddenly demanded, fixing her agreeable eyes upon Winterbourne's.

'Am I grave?' he asked. 'I had an idea I was grinning from ear to ear.'

'You look as if you were taking me to a funeral. If that's a grin, your ears are very near together.'

'Should you like me to dance a hornpipe on the deck?'

'Pray do, and I'll carry round your hat. It will pay the expenses of our journey.'

'I never was better pleased in my life,' murmured Winterbourne.

She looked at him a moment, and then burst into a little laugh. 'I like to make you say those things! You're a queer mixture!'

In the castle, after they had landed, the subjective element decidedly prevailed. Daisy tripped about the vaulted chambers, rustled her skirts in the corkscrew staircases, flirted back with a pretty little cry and a shudder from the edge of the *oubliettes*,[6] and turned a singularly well-shaped ear to everything that Winterbourne told her about the place. But he saw that she cared very little for feudal antiquities, and that the dusky traditions of Chillon made but a slight impression upon her. They had the good fortune to have been able to walk about without other companionship than that of the custodian; and Winterbourne arranged with this functionary that they should not be hurried – that they should linger and pause wherever they chose. The custodian interpreted the bargain generously – Winterbourne, on his side, had been generous – and ended by leaving them quite to themselves. Miss Miller's observations were not remarkable for logical consistency; for anything she wanted to say she was sure to find a pretext. She found a great many pretexts in the rugged embrasures of Chillon for asking Winterbourne sudden questions about himself – his family, his previous history, his tastes, his habits, his intentions – and for supplying information upon corresponding points in her own personality. Of her own tastes, habits and intentions Miss Miller was prepared to give the most definite, and indeed the most favourable, account.

'Well; I hope you know enough!' she said to her companion, after he had told her the history of the unhappy Bonivard.[7] 'I never saw a man that knew so much!' The history of Bonivard had evidently, as they say, gone into one ear and out of the other. But Daisy went on to say that she wished Winterbourne would travel with them and 'go round' with them; they might know something, in that case. 'Don't you want to come and teach Randolph?' she asked. Winterbourne said that nothing could possibly please him so much; but that he had unfortunately other occupations. 'Other occupations? I don't believe it!' said Miss Daisy. 'What do you mean? You are not in business.' The young man admitted that he was not in business; but he had engagements which, even within a day or two, would force him to go back to Geneva. 'Oh, bother!' she said, 'I don't believe it!' and she began to talk about something else. But a few moments later, when he was pointing out to her the pretty design of an antique fireplace, she broke out irrelevantly, 'You don't mean to say you are going back to Geneva?'

'It is a melancholy fact that I shall have to return to Geneva to-morrow.'

'Well, Mr. Winterbourne,' said Daisy; 'I think you're horrid!'

'Oh, don't say such dreadful things!' said Winterbourne –
'just at the last.'

'The last!' cried the young girl; 'I call it the first. I have half
a mind to leave you here and go straight back to the hotel
alone.' And for the next ten minutes she did nothing but call
him horrid. Poor Winterbourne was fairly bewildered; no young
lady had as yet done him the honour to be so agitated by the
announcement of his movements. His companion, after this,
ceased to pay any attention to the curiosities of Chillon or the
beauties of the lake; she opened fire upon the mysterious
charmer in Geneva, whom she appeared to have instantly taken
it for granted that he was hurrying back to see. How did Miss
Daisy Miller know that there was a charmer in Geneva? Winterbourne, who denied the existence of such a person, was quite
unable to discover; and he was divided between amazement at
the rapidity of her induction and amusement at the frankness
of her *persiflage*. She seemed to him, in all this, an extraordinary
mixture of innocence and crudity. 'Does she never allow
you more than three days at a time?' asked Daisy, ironically.
'Doesn't she give you a vacation in summer? There's no one so
hard worked but they can get leave to go off somewhere at this
season. I suppose, if you stay another day, she'll come after you
in the boat. Do wait over till Friday, and I will go down to the
landing to see her arrive!' Winterbourne began to think he had
been wrong to feel disappointed in the temper in which the
young lady had embarked. If he had missed the personal accent,
the personal accent was now making its appearance. It sounded
very distinctly, at last, in her telling him she would stop 'teasing'
him if he would promise her solemnly to come down to Rome
in the winter.

'That's not a difficult promise to make,' said Winterbourne.
'My aunt has taken an apartment in Rome for the winter, and
has already asked me to come and see her.'

'I don't want you to come for your aunt,' said Daisy; 'I want
you to come for me.' And this was the only allusion that the
young man was ever to hear her make to his invidious kins-
woman. He declared that, at any rate, he would certainly come.
After this Daisy stopped teasing. Winterbourne took a carriage,

and they drove back to Vevey in the dusk; the young girl was very quiet.

In the evening Winterbourne mentioned to Mrs. Costello that he had spent the afternoon at Chillon, with Miss Daisy Miller.

'The Americans – of the courier?' asked this lady.

'Ah, happily,' said Winterbourne, 'the courier stayed at home.'

'She went with you all alone?'

'All alone.'

Mrs. Costello sniffed a little at her smelling-bottle. 'And that,' she exclaimed, 'is the young person you wanted me to know!'

III

Winterbourne, who had returned to Geneva the day after his excursion to Chillon, went to Rome towards the end of January. His aunt had been established there for several weeks, and he had received a couple of letters from her. 'Those people you were so devoted to last summer at Vevey have turned up here, courier and all,' she wrote. 'They seem to have made several acquaintances, but the courier continues to be the most *intime*. The young lady, however, is also very intimate with some third-rate Italians, with whom she rackets about in a way that makes much talk. Bring me that pretty novel of Cherbuliez's – "Paule Méré"[1] – and don't come later than the 23rd.'

In the natural course of events, Winterbourne, on arriving in Rome, would presently have ascertained Mrs. Miller's address at the American banker's and have gone to pay his compliments to Miss Daisy. 'After what happened at Vevey I certainly think I may call upon them,' he said to Mrs. Costello.

'If, after what happens – at Vevey and everywhere – you desire to keep up the acquaintance, you are very welcome. Of course a man may know every one. Men are welcome to the privilege!'

'Pray what is it that happens – here, for instance?' Winterbourne demanded.

'The girl goes about alone with her foreigners. As to what happens farther, you must apply elsewhere for information. She has picked up half-a-dozen of the regular Roman fortune-hunters, and she takes them about to people's houses. When she comes to a party she brings with her a gentleman with a good deal of manner and a wonderful moustache.'

'And where is the mother?'

'I haven't the least idea. They are very dreadful people.'

Winterbourne meditated a moment. 'They are very ignorant – very innocent only. Depend upon it they are not bad.'

'They are hopelessly vulgar,' said Mrs. Costello. 'Whether or no being hopelessly vulgar is being "bad" is a question for the metaphysicians. They are bad enough to dislike, at any rate; and for this short life that is quite enough.'

The news that Daisy Miller was surrounded by half-a-dozen wonderful moustaches checked Winterbourne's impulse to go straightway to see her. He had perhaps not definitely flattered himself that he had made an ineffaceable impression upon her heart, but he was annoyed at hearing of a state of affairs so little in harmony with an image that had lately flitted in and out of his own meditations; the image of a very pretty girl looking out of an old Roman window and asking herself urgently when Mr. Winterbourne would arrive. If, however, he determined to wait a little before reminding Miss Miller of his claims to her consideration, he went very soon to call upon two or three other friends. One of these friends was an American lady who had spent several winters at Geneva, where she had placed her children at school. She was a very accomplished woman and she lived in the Via Gregoriana.[2] Winterbourne found her in a little crimson drawing-room, on a third floor; the room was filled with southern sunshine. He had not been there ten minutes when the servant came in, announcing 'Madame Mila!' This announcement was presently followed by the entrance of little Randolph Miller, who stopped in the middle of the room and stood staring at Winterbourne. An instant later his pretty sister crossed the threshold; and then, after a considerable interval, Mrs. Miller slowly advanced.

'I know you!' said Randolph.

'I'm sure you know a great many things,' exclaimed Winterbourne, taking him by the hand. 'How is your education coming on?'

Daisy was exchanging greetings very prettily with her hostess; but when she heard Winterbourne's voice she quickly turned her head. 'Well, I declare!' she said.

'I told you I should come, you know,' Winterbourne rejoined, smiling.

'Well – I didn't believe it,' said Miss Daisy.

'I am much obliged to you,' laughed the young man.

'You might have come to see me!' said Daisy.

'I arrived only yesterday.'

'I don't believe that!' the young girl declared.

Winterbourne turned with a protesting smile to her mother; but this lady evaded his glance, and seating herself, fixed her eyes upon her son. 'We've got a bigger place than this,' said Randolph. 'It's all gold on the walls.'

Mrs. Miller turned uneasily in her chair. 'I told you if I were to bring you, you would say something!' she murmured.

'I told *you*!' Randolph exclaimed. 'I tell *you*, sir!' he added jocosely, giving Winterbourne a thump on the knee. 'It *is* bigger, too!'

Daisy had entered upon a lively conversation with her hostess; Winterbourne judged it becoming to address a few words to her mother. 'I hope you have been well since we parted at Vevey,' he said.

Mrs. Miller now certainly looked at him – at his chin. 'Not very well, sir,' she answered.

'She's got the dyspepsia,' said Randolph. 'I've got it too. Father's got it. I've got it worst!'

This announcement, instead of embarrassing Mrs. Miller, seemed to relieve her. 'I suffer from the liver,' she said. 'I think it's this climate; it's less bracing than Schenectady, especially in the winter season. I don't know whether you know we reside at Schenectady. I was saying to Daisy that I certainly hadn't found any one like Dr. Davis, and I didn't believe I should. Oh, at Schenectady, he stands first; they think everything of him. He has so much to do, and yet there was nothing he wouldn't do for me. He said he never saw anything like my dyspepsia, but he was bound to cure it. I'm sure there was nothing he wouldn't try. He was just going to try something new when we came off. Mr. Miller wanted Daisy to see Europe for herself. But I wrote to Mr. Miller that it seems as if I couldn't get on without Dr. Davis. At Schenectady he stands at the very top; and there's a great deal of sickness there, too. It affects my sleep.'

Winterbourne had a good deal of pathological gossip with Dr. Davis's patient, during which Daisy chattered unremittingly to her own companion. The young man asked Mrs. Miller how she was pleased with Rome. 'Well, I must say I am disappointed,' she answered. 'We had heard so much about it; I suppose we had heard too much. But we couldn't help that. We had been led to expect something different.'

'Ah, wait a little, and you will become very fond of it,' said Winterbourne.

'I hate it worse and worse every day!' cried Randolph.

'You are like the infant Hannibal,'[3] said Winterbourne.

'No, I ain't!' Randolph declared, at a venture.

'You are not much like an infant,' said his mother. 'But we have seen places,' she resumed, 'that I should put a long way before Rome.' And in reply to Winterbourne's interrogation, 'There's Zurich,' she observed; 'I think Zurich is lovely; and we hadn't heard half so much about it.'

'The best place we've seen is the City of Richmond!' said Randolph.

'He means the ship,' his mother explained. 'We crossed in that ship. Randolph had a good time on the City of Richmond.'

'It's the best place I've seen,' the child repeated. 'Only it was turned the wrong way.'

'Well, we've got to turn the right way some time,' said Mrs. Miller, with a little laugh. Winterbourne expressed the hope that her daughter at least found some gratification in Rome, and she declared that Daisy was quite carried away. 'It's on account of the society – the society's splendid. She goes round everywhere; she has made a great number of acquaintances. Of course she goes round more than I do. I must say they have been very sociable; they have taken her right in. And then she knows a great many gentlemen. Oh, she thinks there's nothing like Rome. Of course, it's a great deal pleasanter for a young lady if she knows plenty of gentlemen.'

By this time Daisy had turned her attention again to Winterbourne. 'I've been telling Mrs. Walker how mean you were!' the young girl announced.

'And what is the evidence you have offered?' asked Winterbourne, rather annoyed at Miss Miller's want of appreciation of the zeal of an admirer who on his way down to Rome had stopped neither at Bologna nor at Florence, simply because of a certain sentimental impatience. He remembered that a cynical compatriot had once told him that American women – the pretty ones, and this gave a largeness to the axiom – were at once the most exacting in the world and the least endowed with a sense of indebtedness.

'Why, you were awfully mean at Vevey,' said Daisy. 'You wouldn't do anything. You wouldn't stay there when I asked you.'

'My dearest young lady,' cried Winterbourne, with eloquence, 'have I come all the way to Rome to encounter your reproaches?'

'Just hear him say that!' said Daisy to her hostess, giving a twist to a bow on this lady's dress. 'Did you ever hear anything so quaint?'

'So quaint, my dear?' murmured Mrs. Walker, in the tone of a partisan of Winterbourne.

'Well, I don't know,' said Daisy, fingering Mrs. Walker's ribbons. 'Mrs. Walker, I want to tell you something.'

'Motherr,' interposed Randolph, with his rough ends to his words, 'I tell you you've got to go. Eugenio 'll raise something!'

'I'm not afraid of Eugenio,' said Daisy, with a toss of her head. 'Look here, Mrs. Walker,' she went on, 'you know I'm coming to your party.'

'I am delighted to hear it.'

'I've got a lovely dress.'

'I am very sure of that.'

'But I want to ask a favour – permission to bring a friend.'

'I shall be happy to see any of your friends,' said Mrs. Walker, turning with a smile to Mrs. Miller.

'Oh, they are not my friends,' answered Daisy's mamma, smiling shyly, in her own fashion. 'I never spoke to them!'

'It's an intimate friend of mine – Mr. Giovanelli,' said Daisy, without a tremor in her clear little voice or a shadow on her brilliant little face.

Mrs. Walker was silent a moment, she gave a rapid glance at Winterbourne. 'I shall be glad to see Mr. Giovanelli,' she then said.

'He's an Italian,' Daisy pursued, with the prettiest serenity. 'He's a great friend of mine – he's the handsomest man in the world – except Mr. Winterbourne! He knows plenty of Italians, but he wants to know some Americans. He thinks ever so much of Americans. He's tremendously clever. He's perfectly lovely!'

It was settled that this brilliant personage should be brought to Mrs. Walker's party, and then Mrs. Miller prepared to take her leave. 'I guess we'll go back to the hotel,' she said.

'You may go back to the hotel, mother, but I'm going to take a walk,' said Daisy.

'She's going to walk with Mr. Giovanelli,' Randolph proclaimed.

'I am going to the Pincio,'[4] said Daisy, smiling.

'Alone, my dear – at this hour?' Mrs. Walker asked. The afternoon was drawing to a close – it was the hour for the throng of carriages and of contemplative pedestrians. 'I don't think it's safe, my dear,' said Mrs. Walker.

'Neither do I,' subjoined Mrs. Miller. 'You'll get the fever as sure as you live. Remember what Dr. Davis told you!'

'Give her some medicine before she goes,' said Randolph.

The company had risen to its feet; Daisy, still showing her pretty teeth, bent over and kissed her hostess. 'Mrs. Walker, you are too perfect,' she said. 'I'm not going alone; I am going to meet a friend.'

'Your friend won't keep you from getting the fever,' Mrs. Miller observed.

'Is it Mr. Giovanelli?' asked the hostess.

Winterbourne was watching the young girl; at this question his attention quickened. She stood there smiling and smoothing her bonnet-ribbons; she glanced at Winterbourne. Then, while she glanced and smiled, she answered without a shade of hesitation, 'Mr. Giovanelli – the beautiful Giovanelli.'

'My dear young friend,' said Mrs. Walker, taking her hand, pleadingly, 'don't walk off to the Pincio at this hour to meet a beautiful Italian.'

'Well, he speaks English,' said Mrs. Miller.

'Gracious me!' Daisy exclaimed, 'I don't want to do anything improper. There's an easy way to settle it.' She continued to glance at Winterbourne. 'The Pincio is only a hundred yards distant, and if Mr. Winterbourne were as polite as he pretends he would offer to walk with me!'

Winterbourne's politeness hastened to affirm itself, and the young girl gave him gracious leave to accompany her. They passed down-stairs before her mother, and at the door Winterbourne perceived Mrs. Miller's carriage drawn up, with the ornamental courier whose acquaintance he had made at Vevey seated within. 'Good-bye, Eugenio!' cried Daisy, 'I'm going to take a walk.' The distance from the Via Gregoriana to the beautiful garden at the other end of the Pincian Hill is, in fact, rapidly traversed. As the day was splendid, however, and the concourse of vehicles, walkers, and loungers numerous, the young Americans found their progress much delayed. This fact was highly agreeable to Winterbourne, in spite of his conscious-ness of his singular situation. The slow-moving, idly-gazing Roman crowd bestowed much attention upon the extremely pretty young foreign lady who was passing through it upon his arm; and he wondered what on earth had been in Daisy's mind when she proposed to expose herself, unattended, to its appreciation. His own mission, to her sense, apparently, was to consign her to the hands of Mr. Giovanelli; but Winter-bourne, at once annoyed and gratified, resolved that he would do no such thing.

'Why haven't you been to see me?' asked Daisy. 'You can't get out of that.'

'I have had the honour of telling you that I have only just stepped out of the train.'

'You must have stayed in the train a good while after it stopped!' cried the young girl, with her little laugh. 'I suppose you were asleep. You have had time to go to see Mrs. Walker.'

'I knew Mrs. Walker –' Winterbourne began to explain.

'I knew where you knew her. You knew her at Geneva. She told me so. Well, you knew me at Vevey. That's just as good. So you ought to have come.' She asked him no other question

than this; she began to prattle about her own affairs. 'We'v
got splendid rooms at the hotel; Eugenio says they're the bes
rooms in Rome. We are going to stay all winter – if we don'
die of the fever; and I guess we'll stay then. It's a great deal
nicer than I thought; I thought it would be fearfully quiet; I was
sure it would be awfully poky. I was sure we should be going
round all the time with one of those dreadful old men that
explain about the pictures and things. But we only had about
a week of that, and now I'm enjoying myself. I know ever
so many people, and they are all so charming. The society's
extremely select. There are all kinds – English, and Germans,
and Italians. I think I like the English best. I like their style of
conversation. But there are some lovely Americans. I never saw
anything so hospitable. There's something or other every day.
There's not much dancing; but I must say I never thought
dancing was everything. I was always fond of conversation. I
guess I shall have plenty at Mrs. Walker's – her rooms are so
small.' When they had passed the gate of the Pincian Gardens,
Miss Miller began to wonder where Mr. Giovanelli might be.
'We had better go straight to that place in front,' she said,
'where you look at the view.'

'I certainly shall not help you to find him,' Winterbourne
declared.

'Then I shall find him without you,' said Miss Daisy.

'You certainly won't leave me!' cried Winterbourne.

She burst into her little laugh. 'Are you afraid you'll get lost
– or run over? But there's Giovanelli, leaning against that tree.
He's staring at the women in the carriages: did you ever see
anything so cool?'

Winterbourne perceived at some distance a little man standing with folded arms, nursing his cane. He had a handsome
face, an artfully poised hat, a glass in one eye and a nosegay in
his button-hole. Winterbourne looked at him a moment and
then said, 'Do you mean to speak to that man?'

'Do I mean to speak to him? Why, you don't suppose I mean
to communicate by signs?'

'Pray understand, then,' said Winterbourne, 'that I intend to
remain with you.'

opped and looked at him, without a sign of troubled ness in her face; with nothing but the presence of her eyes and her happy dimples. 'Well, she's a cool one!' the young man.

on't like the way you say that,' said Daisy. 'It's too rious.'

beg your pardon if I say it wrong. The main point is to give a an idea of my meaning.'

The young girl looked at him more gravely, but with eyes that were prettier than ever. 'I have never allowed a gentleman to dictate to me, or to interfere with anything I do.'

'I think you have made a mistake,' said Winterbourne. 'You should sometimes listen to a gentleman – the right one.'

Daisy began to laugh again. 'I do nothing but listen to gentlemen!' she exclaimed. 'Tell me if Mr. Giovanelli is the right one.'

The gentleman with the nosegay in his bosom had now perceived our two friends, and was approaching the young girl with obsequious rapidity. He bowed to Winterbourne as well as to the latter's companion; he had a brilliant smile, an intelligent eye; Winterbourne thought him not a bad-looking fellow. But he nevertheless said to Daisy – 'No, he's not the right one.'

Daisy evidently had a natural talent for performing introductions; she mentioned the name of each of her companions to the other. She strolled along with one of them on each side of her; Mr. Giovanelli, who spoke English very cleverly – Winterbourne afterwards learned that he had practised the idiom upon a great many American heiresses – addressed her a great deal of very polite nonsense; he was extremely urbane, and the young American, who said nothing, reflected upon that profundity of Italian cleverness which enables people to appear more gracious in proportion as they are more acutely disappointed. Giovanelli, of course, had counted upon something more intimate; he had not bargained for a party of three. But he kept his temper in a manner which suggested far-stretching intentions. Winterbourne flattered himself that he had taken his measure. 'He is not a gentleman,' said the young American; 'he is only a clever imitation of one. He is a music-master, or a penny-a-liner, or a third-rate artist. Damn his good looks!' Mr. Giovanelli had certainly a very pretty face; but Winterbourne felt a superior indignation at his own lovely fellow-countrywoman's not knowing the difference between a spurious gentleman and a real one. Giovanelli chattered and jested and made himself wonderfully agreeable. It was true that if he was an imitation the imitation was very skilful. 'Nevertheless,' Winterbourne said to himself, 'a nice girl ought to know!' And then he came back to the question whether this was in fact a nice girl. Would a nice girl – even allowing for her being a little American flirt – make a rendezvous with a presumably low-lived foreigner? The rendezvous in this case, indeed, had been in broad daylight, and in the most crowded corner of Rome; but was it not impossible to regard the choice of these circumstances as a proof of extreme cynicism? Singular though it may seem, Winterbourne was vexed that the young girl, in joining her *amoroso*,[5] should not appear more impatient of his own company, and he was vexed because of his inclination. It was impossible to regard her as a perfectly well-conducted young lady; she was wanting in a certain indispensable delicacy. It would therefore simplify matters greatly to be able to treat her as the object of one of those sentiments which are called by romancers 'lawless passions'. That she should seem to wish to get rid of him would help him to think more lightly of her, and to be able to think more lightly of her would make her much less perplexing. But Daisy, on this occasion, continued to present herself as an inscrutable combination of audacity and innocence.

She had been walking some quarter of an hour, attended by her two cavaliers, and responding in a tone of very childish gaiety, as it seemed to Winterbourne, to the pretty speeches of Mr. Giovanelli, when a carriage that had detached itself from the revolving train drew up beside the path. At the same moment Winterbourne perceived that his friend Mrs. Walker – the lady whose house he had lately left – was seated in the vehicle and was beckoning to him. Leaving Miss Miller's side, he hastened to obey her summons. Mrs. Walker was flushed; she wore an excited air. 'It is really too dreadful,' she said. 'That girl must not do this sort of thing. She must not walk here with you two men. Fifty people have noticed her.'

Winterbourne raised his eyebrows. 'I think it's a pity to make too much fuss about it.'

'It's a pity to let the girl ruin herself!'

'She is very innocent,' said Winterbourne.

'She's very crazy!' cried Mrs. Walker. 'Did you ever see anything so imbecile as her mother? After you had all left me, just now, I could not sit still for thinking of it. It seemed too pitiful, not even to attempt to save her. I ordered the carriage and put on my bonnet, and came here as quickly as possible. Thank heaven I have found you!'

'What do you propose to do with us?' asked Winterbourne, smiling.

'To ask her to get in, to drive her about here for half-an-hour, so that the world may see she is not running absolutely wild, and then to take her safely home.'

'I don't think it's a very happy thought,' said Winterbourne; 'but you can try.'

Mrs. Walker tried. The young man went in pursuit of Miss Miller, who had simply nodded and smiled at his interlocutrix in the carriage and had gone her way with her own companion. Daisy, on learning that Mrs. Walker wished to speak to her, retraced her steps with a perfect good grace and with Mr. Giovanelli at her side. She declared that she was delighted to have a chance to present this gentleman to Mrs. Walker. She immediately achieved the introduction, and declared that she had never in her life seen anything so lovely as Mrs. Walker's carriage-rug.

'I am glad you admire it,' said this lady, smiling sweetly. 'Will you get in and let me put it over you?'

'Oh, no, thank you,' said Daisy. 'I shall admire it much more as I see you driving round with it.'

'Do get in and drive with me,' said Mrs. Walker.

'That would be charming, but it's so enchanting just as I am!' and Daisy gave a brilliant glance at the gentlemen on either side of her.

'It may be enchanting, dear child, but it is not the custom here,' urged Mrs. Walker, leaning forward in her victoria with her hands devoutly clasped.

'Well, it ought to be, then!' said Daisy. 'If I didn't walk I should expire.'

'You should walk with your mother, dear,' cried the lady from Geneva, losing patience.

'With my mother dear!' exclaimed the young girl. Winterbourne saw that she scented interference. 'My mother never walked ten steps in her life. And then, you know,' she added with a laugh, 'I am more than five years old.'

'You are old enough to be more reasonable. You are old enough, dear Miss Miller, to be talked about.'

Daisy looked at Mrs. Walker, smiling intensely. 'Talked about? What do you mean?'

'Come into my carriage and I will tell you.'

Daisy turned her quickened glance again from one of the gentlemen beside her to the other. Mr. Giovanelli was bowing to and fro, rubbing down his gloves and laughing very agreeably; Winterbourne thought it a most unpleasant scene. 'I don't think I want to know what you mean,' said Daisy presently. 'I don't think I should like it.'

Winterbourne wished that Mrs. Walker would tuck in her carriage-rug and drive away; but this lady did not enjoy being defied, as she afterwards told him. 'Should you prefer being thought a very reckless girl?' she demanded.

'Gracious me!' exclaimed Daisy. She looked again at Mr. Giovanelli, then she turned to Winterbourne. There was a little pink flush in her cheek; she was tremendously pretty. 'Does Mr. Winterbourne think,' she asked slowly, smiling, throwing back her head and glancing at him from head to foot, 'that – to save my reputation – I ought to get into the carriage?'

Winterbourne coloured; for an instant he hesitated greatly. It seemed so strange to hear her speak that way of her 'reputation'. But he himself, in fact, must speak in accordance with gallantry. The finest gallantry, here, was simply to tell her the truth; and the truth, for Winterbourne, as the few indications I have been able to give have made him known to the reader, was that Daisy Miller should take Mrs. Walker's advice. He looked at her exquisite prettiness; and then he said very gently, 'I think you should get into the carriage.'

Daisy gave a violent laugh. 'I never heard anything so stiff! If this is improper, Mrs. Walker,' she pursued, 'then I am all improper, and you must give me up. Good-bye; I hope you'll have a lovely ride!' and, with Mr. Giovanelli, who made a triumphantly obsequious salute, she turned away.

Mrs. Walker sat looking after her, and there were tears in Mrs. Walker's eyes. 'Get in here, sir,' she said to Winterbourne, indicating the place beside her. The young man answered that he felt bound to accompany Miss Miller; whereupon Mrs. Walker declared that if he refused her this favour she would never speak to him again. She was evidently in earnest. Winterbourne overtook Daisy and her companion and, offering the young girl his hand, told her that Mrs. Walker had made an imperious claim upon his society. He expected that in answer she would say something rather free, something to commit herself still farther to that 'recklessness' from which Mrs. Walker had so charitably endeavoured to dissuade her. But she only shook his hand, hardly looking at him, while Mr. Giovanelli bade him farewell with a too emphatic flourish of the hat.

Winterbourne was not in the best possible humour as he took his seat in Mrs. Walker's victoria. 'That was not clever of you,' he said candidly, while the vehicle mingled again with the throng of carriages.

'In such a case,' his companion answered, 'I don't wish to be clever, I wish to be *earnest*!'

'Well, your earnestness has only offended her and put her off.'

'It has happened very well,' said Mrs. Walker. 'If she is so perfectly determined to compromise herself, the sooner one knows it the better; one can act accordingly.'

'I suspect she meant no harm,' Winterbourne rejoined.

'So I thought a month ago. But she has been going too far.'

'What has she been doing?'

'Everything that is not done here. Flirting with any man she could pick up; sitting in corners with mysterious Italians; dancing all the evening with the same partners; receiving visits at eleven o'clock at night. Her mother goes away when visitors come.'

'But her brother,' said Winterbourne, laughing, 'sits up till midnight.'

'He must be edified by what he sees. I'm told that at their hotel every one is talking about her, and that a smile goes round among the servants when a gentleman comes and asks for Miss Miller.'

'The servants be hanged!' said Winterbourne angrily. 'The poor girl's only fault,' he presently added, 'is that she is very uncultivated.'

'She is naturally indelicate,' Mrs. Walker declared. 'Take that example this morning. How long had you known her at Vevey?'

'A couple of days.'

'Fancy, then, her making it a personal matter that you should have left the place!'

Winterbourne was silent for some moments; then he said, 'I suspect, Mrs. Walker, that you and I have lived too long at Geneva!' And he added a request that she should inform him with what particular design she had made him enter her carriage.

'I wished to beg you to cease your relations with Miss Miller – not to flirt with her – to give her no farther opportunity to expose herself – to let her alone, in short.'

'I'm afraid I can't do that,' said Winterbourne. 'I like her extremely.'

'All the more reason that you shouldn't help her to make a scandal.'

'There shall be nothing scandalous in my attentions to her.'

'There certainly will be in the way she takes them. But I have said what I had on my conscience,' Mrs. Walker pursued. 'If you wish to rejoin the young lady I will put you down. Here, by-the-way, you have a chance.'

The carriage was traversing that part of the Pincian Garden which overhangs the wall of Rome and overlooks the beautiful Villa Borghese.[6] It is bordered by a large parapet, near which there are several seats. One of the seats, at a distance, was occupied by a gentleman and a lady, towards whom Mrs. Walker gave a toss of her head. At the same moment these persons rose and walked towards the parapet. Winterbourne

had asked the coachman to stop; he now descended from the
carriage. His companion looked at him a moment in silence;
then, while he raised his hat, she drove majestically away.
Winterbourne stood there; he had turned his eyes towards Daisy
and her cavalier. They evidently saw no one; they were too
deeply occupied with each other. When they reached the low
garden-wall they stood a moment looking off at the great flat-
topped pine-clusters of the Villa Borghese; then Giovanelli
seated himself familiarly upon the broad ledge of the wall. The
western sun in the opposite sky sent out a brilliant shaft through
a couple of cloud-bars; whereupon Daisy's companion took her
parasol out of her hands and opened it. She came a little nearer
and he held the parasol over her; then, still holding it, he let it
rest upon her shoulder, so that both of their heads were hidden
from Winterbourne. This young man lingered a moment, then
he began to walk. But he walked – not towards the couple with
the parasol; towards the residence of his aunt, Mrs. Costello.

IV

He flattered himself on the following day that there was no smiling among the servants when he, at least, asked for Mrs. Miller at her hotel. This lady and her daughter, however, were not at home; and on the next day after, repeating his visit, Winterbourne again had the misfortune not to find them. Mrs. Walker's party took place on the evening of the third day, and in spite of the frigidity of his last interview with the hostess Winterbourne was among the guests. Mrs. Walker was one of those American ladies who, while residing abroad, make a point, in their own phrase, of studying European society; and she had on this occasion collected several specimens of her diversely-born fellow-mortals to serve, as it were, as text-books. When Winterbourne arrived Daisy Miller was not there; but in a few moments he saw her mother come in alone, very shyly and ruefully. Mrs. Miller's hair, above her exposed-looking temples, was more frizzled than ever. As she approached Mrs. Walker, Winterbourne also drew near.

'You see I've come all alone,' said poor Mrs. Miller. 'I'm so frightened; I don't know what to do; it's the first time I've ever been to a party alone – especially in this country. I wanted to bring Randolph or Eugenio, or some one, but Daisy just pushed me off by myself. I ain't used to going round alone.'

'And does not your daughter intend to favour us with her society?' demanded Mrs. Walker, impressively.

'Well, Daisy's all dressed,' said Mrs. Miller, with that accent of the dispassionate, if not of the philosophic, historian with which she always recorded the current incidents of her daughter's career. 'She got dressed on purpose before dinner. But she's got a friend of hers there; that gentleman – the Italian – that she wanted to bring. They've got going at the piano; it seems as if they couldn't leave off. Mr. Giovanelli sings splendidly. But I guess they'll come before very long,' concluded Mrs. Miller hopefully.

'I'm sorry she should come – in that way,' said Mrs. Walker.

'Well, I told her that there was no use in her getting dressed before dinner if she was going to wait three hours,' responded Daisy's mamma. 'I didn't see the use of her putting on such a dress as that to sit round with Mr. Giovanelli.'

'This is most horrible!' said Mrs. Walker, turning away and addressing herself to Winterbourne. '*Elle s'affiche.*[1] It's her revenge for my having ventured to remonstrate with her. When she comes I shall not speak to her.'

Daisy came after eleven o'clock, but she was not, on such an occasion, a young lady to wait to be spoken to. She rustled forward in radiant loveliness, smiling and chattering, carrying a large bouquet and attended by Mr. Giovanelli. Every one stopped talking, and turned and looked at her. She came straight to Mrs. Walker. 'I'm afraid you thought I never was coming, so I sent mother off to tell you. I wanted to make Mr. Giovanelli practise some things before he came; you know he sings beautifully, and I want you to ask him to sing. This is Mr. Giovanelli; you know I introduced him to you; he's got the most lovely voice and he knows the most charming set of songs. I made him go over them this evening, on purpose; we had the greatest time at the hotel.' Of all this Daisy delivered herself with the sweetest, brightest audibleness, looking now at her hostess and now round the room, while she gave a series of little pats, round her shoulders, to the edges of her dress. 'Is there any one I know?' she asked.

'I think every one knows you!' said Mrs. Walker pregnantly, and she gave a very cursory greeting to Mr. Giovanelli. This gentleman bore himself gallantly. He smiled and bowed and showed his white teeth, he curled his moustaches and rolled his eyes, and performed all the proper functions of a handsome Italian at an evening party. He sang, very prettily, half-a-dozen songs, though Mrs. Walker afterwards declared that she had been quite unable to find out who asked him. It was apparently not Daisy who had given him his orders. Daisy sat at a distance from the piano, and though she had publicly, as it were, professed a high admiration for his singing, talked, not inaudibly, while it was going on.

'It's a pity these rooms are so small; we can't dance,' she said to Winterbourne, as if she had seen him five minutes before.

'I am not sorry we can't dance,' Winterbourne answered; 'I don't dance.'

'Of course you don't dance; you're too stiff,' said Miss Daisy. 'I hope you enjoyed your drive with Mrs. Walker.'

'No, I didn't enjoy it; I preferred walking with you.'

'We paired off, that was much better,' said Daisy. 'But did you ever hear anything so cool as Mrs. Walker's wanting me to get into her carriage and drop poor Mr. Giovanelli; and under the pretext that it was proper? People have different ideas! It would have been most unkind; he had been talking about that walk for ten days.'

'He should not have talked about it at all,' said Winterbourne; 'he would never have proposed to a young lady of this country to walk about the streets with him.'

'About the streets?' cried Daisy, with her pretty stare. 'Where then would he have proposed to her to walk? The Pincio is not the streets, either; and I, thank goodness, am not a young lady of this country. The young ladies of this country have a dreadfully poky time of it, so far as I can learn; I don't see why I should change my habits for *them*.'

'I am afraid your habits are those of a flirt,' said Winterbourne gravely.

'Of course they are,' she cried, giving him her little smiling stare again. 'I'm a fearful, frightful flirt! Did you ever hear of a nice girl that was not? But I suppose you will tell me now that I am not a nice girl.'

'You're a very nice girl, but I wish you would flirt with me, and me only,' said Winterbourne.

'Ah! Thank you, thank you very much; you are the last man I should think of flirting with. As I have had the pleasure of informing you, you are too stiff.'

'You say that too often,' said Winterbourne.

Daisy gave a delighted laugh. 'If I could have the sweet hope of making you angry, I would say it again.'

'Don't do that; when I am angry I'm stiffer than ever. But if you won't flirt with me, do cease at least to flirt with your friend at the piano; they don't understand that sort of thing here.'

'I thought they understood nothing else!' exclaimed Daisy.

'Not in young unmarried women.'

'It seems to me much more proper in young unmarried women than in old married ones,' Daisy declared.

'Well,' said Winterbourne, 'when you deal with natives you must go by the custom of the place. Flirting is a purely American custom; it doesn't exist here. So when you show yourself in public with Mr. Giovanelli and without your mother –'

'Gracious! poor mother!' interposed Daisy.

'Though you may be flirting, Mr. Giovanelli is not; he means something else.'

'He isn't preaching, at any rate,' said Daisy with vivacity. 'And if you want very much to know, we are neither of us flirting; we are too good friends for that; we are very intimate friends.'

'Ah!' rejoined Winterbourne, 'if you are in love with each other it is another affair.'

She had allowed him up to this point to talk so frankly that he had no expectation of shocking her by this ejaculation; but she immediately got up, blushing visibly, and leaving him to exclaim mentally that little American flirts were the queerest creatures in the world. 'Mr. Giovanelli, at least,' she said, giving her interlocutor a single glance, 'never says such very disagreeable things to me.'

Winterbourne was bewildered; he stood staring. Mr. Giovanelli had finished singing; he left the piano and came over to Daisy. 'Won't you come into the other room and have some tea?' he asked, bending before her with his decorative smile.

Daisy turned to Winterbourne, beginning to smile again. He was still more perplexed, for this inconsequent smile made nothing clear, though it seemed to prove, indeed, that she had a sweetness and softness that reverted instinctively to the pardon of offences. 'It has never occurred to Mr. Winterbourne to offer me any tea,' she said, with her little tormenting manner.

'I have offered you advice,' Winterbourne rejoined.

'I prefer weak tea!' cried Daisy, and she went off with the brilliant Giovanelli. She sat with him in the adjoining room, in the embrasure of the window, for the rest of the evening. There was an interesting performance at the piano, but neither of these young people gave heed to it. When Daisy came to take leave of Mrs. Walker, this lady conscientiously repaired the weakness of which she had been guilty at the moment of the young girl's arrival. She turned her back straight upon Miss Miller and left her to depart with what grace she might. Winterbourne was standing near the door; he saw it all. Daisy turned very pale and looked at her mother, but Mrs. Miller was humbly unconscious of any violation of the usual social forms. She appeared, indeed, to have felt an incongruous impulse to draw attention to her own striking observance of them. 'Good night, Mrs. Walker,' she said; 'we've had a beautiful evening. You see if I let Daisy come to parties without me, I don't want her to go away without me.' Daisy turned away, looking with a pale, grave face at the circle near the door; Winterbourne saw that, for the first moment, she was too much shocked and puzzled even for indignation. He on his side was greatly touched.

'That was very cruel,' he said to Mrs. Walker.

'She never enters my drawing-room again,' replied his hostess.

Since Winterbourne was not to meet her in Mrs. Walker's drawing-room, he went as often as possible to Mrs. Miller's hotel. The ladies were rarely at home, but when he found them the devoted Giovanelli was always present. Very often the polished little Roman was in the drawing-room with Daisy alone, Mrs. Miller being apparently constantly of the opinion that discretion is the better part of surveillance. Winterbourne noted, at first with surprise, that Daisy on these occasions was never embarrassed or annoyed by his own entrance; but he very presently began to feel that she had no more surprises for him; the unexpected in her behaviour was the only thing to expect.

She showed no displeasure at her *tête-à-tête* with Giovanelli
being interrupted; she could chatter as freshly and freely with
two gentlemen as with one; there was always in her conversation, the same odd mixture of audacity and puerility. Winterbourne remarked to himself that if she was seriously interested
in Giovanelli it was very singular that she should not take more
trouble to preserve the sanctity of their interviews, and he liked
her the more for her innocent-looking indifference and her
apparently inexhaustible good humour. He could hardly have
said why, but she seemed to him a girl who would never be
jealous. At the risk of exciting a somewhat derisive smile on
the reader's part, I may affirm that with regard to the women
who had hitherto interested him it very often seemed to Winterbourne among the possibilities that, given certain contingencies,
he should be afraid – literally afraid – of these ladies. He had a
pleasant sense that he should never be afraid of Daisy Miller.
It must be added that this sentiment was not altogether flattering
to Daisy; it was part of his conviction, or rather of his apprehension, that she would prove a very light young person.

But she was evidently very much interested in Giovanelli. She
looked at him whenever he spoke; she was perpetually telling
him to do this and to do that; she was constantly 'chaffing'
and abusing him. She appeared completely to have forgotten
that Winterbourne had said anything to displease her at Mrs.
Walker's little party. One Sunday afternoon, having gone to St.
Peter's[2] with his aunt, Winterbourne perceived Daisy strolling
about the great church in company with the inevitable Giovanelli. Presently he pointed out the young girl and her cavalier
to Mrs. Costello. This lady looked at them a moment through
her eyeglass, and then she said:

'That's what makes you so pensive in these days, eh?'

'I had not the least idea I was pensive,' said the young man.

'You are very much pre-occupied, you are thinking of
something.'

'And what is it,' he asked, 'that you accuse me of thinking
of?'

'Of that young lady's – Miss Baker's, Miss Chandler's –

what's her name? – Miss Miller's intrigue with that little
barber's block.'[3]

'Do you call it an intrigue,' Winterbourne asked – 'an affair
that goes on with such peculiar publicity?'

'That's their folly,' said Mrs. Costello, 'it's not their merit.'

'No,' rejoined Winterbourne, with something of that pen-
siveness to which his aunt had alluded. 'I don't believe that
there is anything to be called an intrigue.'

'I have heard a dozen people speak of it; they say she is quite
carried away by him.'

'They are certainly very intimate,' said Winterbourne.

Mrs. Costello inspected the young couple again with her
optical instrument. 'He is very handsome. One easily sees how
it is. She thinks him the most elegant man in the world, the
finest gentleman. She has never seen anything like him; he is
better even than the courier. It was the courier probably who
introduced him, and if he succeeds in marrying the young lady,
the courier will come in for a magnificent commission.'

'I don't believe she thinks of marrying him,' said Winterbourne, 'and I don't believe he hopes to marry her.'

'You may be very sure she thinks of nothing. She goes on
from day to day, from hour to hour, as they did in the Golden
Age.[4] I can imagine nothing more vulgar. And at the same time,'
added Mrs. Costello, 'depend upon it that she may tell you any
moment that she is "engaged".'

'I think that is more than Giovanelli expects,' said Winterbourne.

'Who is Giovanelli?'

'The little Italian. I have asked questions about him and
learned something. He is apparently a perfectly respectable little
man. I believe he is in a small way a *cavaliere avvocato*.[5] But
he doesn't move in what are called the first circles. I think it is
really not absolutely impossible that the courier introduced
him. He is evidently immensely charmed with Miss Miller. If
she thinks him the finest gentleman in the world, he, on his
side, has never found himself in personal contact with such
splendour, such opulence, such expensiveness, as this young

lady's. And then she must seem to him wonderfully pretty and interesting. I rather doubt whether he dreams of marrying her. That must appear to him too impossible a piece of luck. He has nothing but his handsome face to offer, and there is a substantial Mr. Miller in that mysterious land of dollars. Giovanelli knows that he hasn't a title to offer. If he were only a count or a *marchese*!⁶ He must wonder at his luck at the way they have taken him up.'

'He accounts for it by his handsome face, and thinks Miss Miller a young lady *qui se passe ses fantaisies*!⁷ said Mrs. Costello.

'It is very true,' Winterbourne pursued, 'that Daisy and her mamma have not yet risen to that stage of – what shall I call it? – of culture, at which the idea of catching a count or a *marchese* begins. I believe that they are intellectually incapable of that conception.'

'Ah! but the *cavaliere* can't believe it,' said Mrs. Costello.

Of the observation excited by Daisy's 'intrigue', Winterbourne gathered that day at St. Peter's sufficient evidence. A dozen of the American colonists in Rome came to talk with Mrs. Costello, who sat on a little portable stool at the base of one of the great pilasters. The vesper-service was going forward in splendid chants and organ-tones in the adjacent choir, and meanwhile, between Mrs. Costello and her friends, there was a great deal said about poor little Miss Miller's going really 'too far'. Winterbourne was not pleased with what he heard; but when, coming out upon the great steps of the church, he saw Daisy, who had emerged before him, get into an open cab with her accomplice and roll away through the cynical streets of Rome, he could not deny to himself that she was going very far indeed. He felt very sorry for her – not exactly that he believed that she had completely lost her head, but because it was painful to hear so much that was pretty and undefended and natural assigned to a vulgar place among the categories of disorder. He made an attempt after this to give a hint to Mrs. Miller. He met one day in the Corso a friend – a tourist like himself – who had just come out of the Doria Palace,⁸ where he had been walking through the beautiful gallery. His friend talked for a moment about the superb portrait of Innocent X. by Velasquez,[9] which hangs in one of the cabinets of the palace, and then said, 'And in the same cabinet, by-the-way, I had the pleasure of contemplating a picture of a different kind – that pretty American girl whom you pointed out to me last week.' In answer to Winterbourne's inquiries, his friend narrated that the pretty American girl – prettier than ever – was seated with a companion in the secluded nook in which the great papal portrait is enshrined.

'Who was her companion?' asked Winterbourne.

'A little Italian with a bouquet in his button-hole. The girl is delightfully pretty, but I thought I understood from you the other day that she was a young lady *du meilleur monde*.'[10]

'So she is!' answered Winterbourne; and having assured himself that his informant had seen Daisy and her companion but five minutes before, he jumped into a cab and went to call on Mrs. Miller. She was at home; but she apologized to him for receiving him in Daisy's absence.

'She's gone out somewhere with Mr. Giovanelli,' said Mrs. Miller. 'She's always going round with Mr. Giovanelli.'

'I have noticed that they are very intimate,' Winterbourne observed.

'Oh! it seems as if they couldn't live without each other!' said Mrs. Miller. 'Well, he's a real gentleman, anyhow. I keep telling Daisy she's engaged!'

'And what does Daisy say?'

'Oh, she says she isn't engaged. But she might as well be!' this impartial parent resumed. 'She goes on as if she was. But I've made Mr. Giovanelli promise to tell me, if *she* doesn't. I should want to write to Mr. Miller about it – shouldn't you?'

Winterbourne replied that he certainly should; and the state of mind of Daisy's mamma struck him as so unprecedented in the annals of parental vigilance that he gave up as utterly irrelevant the attempt to place her upon her guard.

After this Daisy was never at home, and Winterbourne ceased to meet her at the houses of their common acquaintance, because, as he perceived, these shrewd people had quite made up their minds that she was going too far. They ceased to invite

her, and they intimated that they desired to express to observant
Europeans the great truth that, though Miss Daisy Miller was
a young American lady, her behaviour was not representative
– was regarded by her compatriots as abnormal. Winterbourne
wondered how she felt about all the cold shoulders that were
turned towards her, and sometimes it annoyed him to suspect
that she did not feel at all. He said to himself that she was
too light and childish, too uncultivated and unreasoning, too
provincial, to have reflected upon her ostracism or even to have
perceived it. Then at other moments he believed that she carried
about in her elegant and irresponsible little organism a defiant,
passionate, perfectly observant consciousness of the impression
she produced. He asked himself whether Daisy's defiance came
from the consciousness of innocence or from her being, essentially, a young person of the reckless class. It must be admitted
that holding oneself to a belief in Daisy's 'innocence' came to
seem to Winterbourne more and more a matter of fine-spun
gallantry. As I have already had occasion to relate, he was angry
at finding himself reduced to chopping logic about this young
lady; he was vexed at his want of instinctive certitude as to how
far her eccentricities were generic, national, and how far they
were personal. From either view of them he had somehow
missed her, and now it was too late. She was 'carried away' by
Mr. Giovanelli.

A few days after his brief interview with her mother, he
encountered her in that beautiful abode of flowering desolation
known as the Palace of the Caesars.[11] The early Roman spring
had filled the air with bloom and perfume, and the rugged
surface of the Palatine was muffled with tender verdure. Daisy
was strolling along the top of one of those great mounds of
ruin that are embanked with mossy marble and paved with
monumental inscriptions. It seemed to him that Rome had
never been so lovely as just then. He stood looking off at the
enchanting harmony of line and colour that remotely encircles
the city, inhaling the softly humid odours and feeling the fresh-
ness of the year and the antiquity of the place reaffirm themselves in mysterious interfusion. It seemed to him also that Daisy
had never looked so pretty; but this had been an observation

of his whenever he met her. Giovanelli was at her side, and
Giovanelli, too, wore an aspect of even unwonted brilliancy.

'Well,' said Daisy, 'I should think you would be lonesome!'

'Lonesome?' asked Winterbourne.

'You are always going round by yourself. Can't you get any
one to walk with you?'

'I am not so fortunate,' said Winterbourne, 'as your
companion.'

Giovanelli, from the first, had treated Winterbourne with
distinguished politeness; he listened with a deferential air to
his remarks; he laughed, punctiliously, at his pleasantries; he
seemed disposed to testify to his belief that Winterbourne was
a superior young man. He carried himself in no degree like a
jealous wooer; he had obviously a great deal of tact; he had no
objection to your expecting a little humility of him. It even
seemed to Winterbourne at times that Giovanelli would find a
certain mental relief in being able to have a private understanding with him – to say to him, as an intelligent man, that, bless
you, *he* knew how extraordinary was this young lady, and
didn't flatter himself with delusive – or at least *too* delusive –
hopes of matrimony and dollars. On this occasion he strolled
away from his companion to pluck a sprig of almond blossom,
which he carefully arranged in his button-hole.

'I know why you say that,' said Daisy, watching Giovanelli.
'Because you think I go round too much with *him*!' And she
nodded at her attendant.

'Every one thinks so – if you care to know,' said Winterbourne.

'Of course I care to know!' Daisy exclaimed seriously. 'But I
don't believe it. They are only pretending to be shocked. They
don't really care a straw what I do. Besides, I don't go round
so much.'

'I think you will find they do care. They will show it –
disagreeably.'

Daisy looked at him a moment. 'How – disagreeably?'

'Haven't you noticed anything?' Winterbourne asked.

'I have noticed you. But I noticed you were as stiff as an
umbrella the first time I saw you.'

'You will find I am not so stiff as several others,' said Winterbourne, smiling.

'How shall I find it?'

'By going to see the others.'

'What will they do to me?'

'They will give you the cold shoulder. Do you know what that means?'

Daisy was looking at him intently; she began to colour. 'Do you mean as Mrs. Walker did the other night?'

'Exactly!' said Winterbourne.

She looked away at Giovanelli, who was decorating himself with his almond-blossom. Then looking back at Winterbourne – 'I shouldn't think you would let people be so unkind!' she said.

'How can I help it?' he asked.

'I should think you would say something.'

'I do say something;' and he paused a moment. 'I say that your mother tells me that she believes you are engaged.'

'Well, she does,' said Daisy very simply.

Winterbourne began to laugh. 'And does Randolph believe it?' he asked.

'I guess Randolph doesn't believe anything,' said Daisy. Randolph's scepticism excited Winterbourne to farther hilarity, and he observed that Giovanelli was coming back to them. Daisy, observing it too, addressed herself again to her countryman. 'Since you have mentioned it,' she said, 'I *am* engaged.' . . . Winterbourne looked at her; he had stopped laughing. 'You don't believe it!' she added.

He was silent a moment; and then, 'Yes, I believe it!' he said.

'Oh, no, you don't,' she answered. 'Well, then – I am not!'

The young girl and her cicerone were on their way to the gate of the enclosure, so that Winterbourne, who had but lately entered, presently took leave of them. A week afterwards he went to dine at a beautiful villa on the Caelian Hill,[12] and, on arriving, dismissed his hired vehicle. The evening was charming, and he promised himself the satisfaction of walking home beneath the Arch of Constantine[13] and past the vaguely-lighted monuments of the Forum.[14] There was a waning moon in the sky, and her radiance was not brilliant, but she was veiled in a thin cloud-curtain which seemed to diffuse and equalize it. When, on his return from the villa (it was eleven o'clock), Winterbourne approached the dusky circle of the Colosseum,[15] it occurred to him, as a lover of the picturesque, that the interior, in the pale moonshine, would be well worth a glance. He turned aside and walked to one of the empty arches, near which, as he observed, an open carriage – one of the little Roman street-cabs – was stationed. Then he passed in among the cavernous shadows of the great structure, and emerged upon the clear and silent arena. The place had never seemed to him more impressive. One-half of the gigantic circus was in deep shade; the other was sleeping in the luminous dusk. As he stood there he began to murmur Byron's famous lines, out of 'Manfred';[16] but before he had finished his quotation he remembered that if nocturnal meditations in the Colosseum are recommended by the poets, they are deprecated by the doctors. The historic atmosphere was there, certainly; but the historic atmosphere, scientifically considered, was no better than a villainous miasma. Winterbourne walked to the middle of the arena, to take a more general glance, intending thereafter to make a hasty retreat. The great cross in the centre was covered with shadow; it was only as he drew near it that he made it out distinctly. Then he saw that two persons were stationed upon the low steps which formed its base. One of these was a woman, seated; her companion was standing in front of her.

Presently the sound of the woman's voice came to him distinctly in the warm night-air. 'Well, he looks at us as one of the old lions or tigers may have looked at the Christian martyrs!' These were the words he heard, in the familiar accent of Miss Daisy Miller.

'Let us hope he is not very hungry,' responded the ingenious Giovanelli. 'He will have to take me first; you will serve for dessert!'

Winterbourne stopped, with a sort of horror; and, it must be added, with a sort of relief. It was as if a sudden illumination had been flashed upon the ambiguity of Daisy's behaviour and the riddle had become easy to read. She was a young lady whom a gentleman need no longer be at pains to respect. He stood there looking at her – looking at her companion, and not reflecting that though he saw them vaguely, he himself must have been more brightly visible. He felt angry with himself that he had bothered so much about the right way of regarding Miss Daisy Miller. Then, as he was going to advance again, he checked himself; not from the fear that he was doing her injustice, but from a sense of the danger of appearing unbecomingly exhilarated by this sudden revulsion from cautious criticism. He turned away towards the entrance of the place; but as he did so he heard Daisy speak again.

'Why, it was Mr. Winterbourne! He saw me – and he cuts me!'

What a clever little reprobate she was, and how smartly she played an injured innocence! But he wouldn't cut her. Winterbourne came forward again, and went towards the great cross. Daisy had got up; Giovanelli lifted his hat. Winterbourne had now begun to think simply of the craziness, from a sanitary point of view, of a delicate young girl lounging away the evening in this nest of malaria. What if she *were* a clever little reprobate? that was no reason for her dying of the *perniciosa*.[17] 'How long have you been here?' he asked, almost brutally.

Daisy, lovely in the flattering moonlight, looked at him a moment. Then – 'All the evening,' she answered gently . . . 'I never saw anything so pretty.'

'I am afraid,' said Winterbourne, 'that you will not think Roman fever very pretty. This is the way people catch it. I wonder,' he added, turning to Giovanelli, 'that you, a native Roman, should countenance such a terrible indiscretion.'

'Ah,' said the handsome native, 'for myself, I am not afraid.'

'Neither am I – for you! I am speaking for this young lady.'

Giovanelli lifted his well-shaped eyebrows and showed his brilliant teeth. But he took Winterbourne's rebuke with docility. 'I told the Signorina it was a grave indiscretion; but when was the Signorina ever prudent?'

'I never was sick, and I don't mean to be!' the Signorina declared. 'I don't look like much, but I'm healthy! I was bound to see the Colosseum by moonlight; I shouldn't have wanted to go home without that; and we have had the most beautiful time, haven't we, Mr. Giovanelli? If there has been any danger, Eugenio can give me some pills. He has got some splendid pills.'

'I should advise you,' said Winterbourne, 'to drive home as fast as possible and take one!'

'What you say is very wise,' Giovanelli rejoined. 'I will go and make sure the carriage is at hand.' And he went forward rapidly.

Daisy followed with Winterbourne. He kept looking at her; she seemed not in the least embarrassed. Winterbourne said nothing; Daisy chattered about the beauty of the place. 'Well, I *have* seen the Colosseum by moonlight!' she exclaimed. 'That's one good thing.' Then, noticing Winterbourne's silence, she asked him why he didn't speak. He made no answer; he only began to laugh. They passed under one of the dark archways; Giovanelli was in front with the carriage. Here Daisy stopped a moment, looking at the young American. '*Did* you believe I was engaged the other day?' she asked.

'It doesn't matter what I believed the other day,' said Winterbourne, still laughing.

'Well, what do you believe now?'

'I believe that it makes very little difference whether you are engaged or not!'

He felt the young girl's pretty eyes fixed upon him through the thick gloom of the archway; she was apparently going to answer. But Giovanelli hurried her forward. 'Quick, quick,' he said; 'if we get in by midnight we are quite safe.'

Daisy took her seat in the carriage, and the fortunate Italian placed himself beside her. 'Don't forget Eugenio's pills!' said Winterbourne, as he lifted his hat.

'I don't care,' said Daisy, in a little strange tone, 'whether I have Roman fever or not!' Upon this the cab-driver cracked his whip, and they rolled away over the desultory patches of the antique pavement.

Winterbourne – to do him justice, as it were – mentioned to no one that he had encountered Miss Miller, at midnight, in the Colosseum with a gentleman; but nevertheless, a couple of days later, the fact of her having been there under these circumstances was known to every member of the little American circle, and commented accordingly. Winterbourne reflected that they had of course known it at the hotel, and that, after Daisy's return, there had been an exchange of jokes between the porter and the cab-driver. But the young man was conscious at the same moment that it had ceased to be a matter of serious regret to him that the little American flirt should be 'talked about' by low-minded menials. These people, a day or two later, had serious information to give: the little American flirt was alarmingly ill. Winterbourne, when the rumour came to him, immediately went to the hotel for more news. He found that two or three charitable friends had preceded him, and that they were being entertained in Mrs. Miller's salon by Randolph.

'It's going round at night,' said Randolph – 'that's what made her sick. She's always going round at night. I shouldn't think she'd want to – it's so plaguey dark. You can't see anything here at night, except when there's a moon. In America there's always a moon!' Mrs. Miller was invisible; she was now, at least, giving her daughter the advantage of her society. It was evident that Daisy was dangerously ill.

Winterbourne went often to ask for news of her, and once he saw Mrs. Miller, who, though deeply alarmed, was – rather to his surprise – perfectly composed, and, as it appeared, a most efficient and judicious nurse. She talked a good deal about Dr. Davis, but Winterbourne paid her the compliment of saying to himself that she was not, after all, such a monstrous goose. 'Daisy spoke of you the other day,' she said to him. 'Half the time she doesn't know what she's saying, but that time I think she did. She gave me a message; she told me to tell you. She told me to tell you that she never was engaged to that handsome Italian. I am sure I am very glad; Mr. Giovanelli hasn't been near us since she was taken ill. I thought he was so much of a gentleman; but I don't call that very polite! A lady told me that he was afraid I was angry with him for taking Daisy round at night. Well, so I am; but I suppose he knows I'm a lady. I would scorn to scold him. Any way, she says she's not engaged. I don't know why she wanted you to know; but she said to me three times – "Mind you tell Mr. Winterbourne." And then she told me to ask if you remembered the time you went to that castle, in Switzerland. But I said I wouldn't give any such messages as that. Only, if she is not engaged, I'm sure I'm glad to know it.'

But, as Winterbourne had said, it mattered very little. A week after this the poor girl died; it had been a terrible case of the fever. Daisy's grave was in the little Protestant cemetery, in an angle of the wall of imperial Rome, beneath the cypresses and the thick spring-flowers. Winterbourne stood there beside it, with a number of other mourners; a number larger than the scandal excited by the young lady's career would have led you to expect. Near him stood Giovanelli, who came nearer still before Winterbourne turned away. Giovanelli was very pale; on this occasion he had no flower in his button-hole; he seemed to wish to say something. At last he said, 'She was the most beautiful young lady I ever saw, and the most amiable.' And then he added in a moment, 'And she was the most innocent.'

Winterbourne looked at him, and presently repeated his words, 'And the most innocent?'

'The most innocent!'

Winterbourne felt sore and angry. 'Why the devil,' he asked, 'did you take take her to that fatal place?'

Mr. Giovanelli's urbanity was apparently imperturbable. He looked on the ground a moment, and then he said, 'For myself, I had no fear; and she wanted to go.'

'That was no reason!' Winterbourne declared.

The subtle Roman again dropped his eyes. 'If she had lived, I should have got nothing. She would never have married me, I am sure.'

'She would never have married you?'

'For a moment I hoped so. But no. I am sure.'

Winterbourne listened to him; he stood staring at the raw protuberance among the April daisies. When he turned away again Mr. Giovanelli, with his light slow step, had retired.

Winterbourne almost immediately left Rome; but the following summer he again met his aunt, Mrs. Costello, at Vevey. Mrs. Costello was fond of Vevey. In the interval Winterbourne had often thought of Daisy Miller and her mystifying manners.

One day he spoke of her to his aunt – said it was on his conscience that he had done her injustice.

'I am sure I don't know,' said Mrs. Costello. 'How did your injustice affect her?'

'She sent me a message before her death which I didn't understand at the time. But I have understood it since. She would have appreciated one's esteem.'

'Is that a modest way,' asked Mrs. Costello, 'of saying that she would have reciprocated one's affection?'

Winterbourne offered no answer to this question; but he presently said, 'You were right in that remark that you made last summer. I was booked to make a mistake. I have lived too long in foreign parts.'

Nevertheless, he went back to live at Geneva, whence there continue to come the most contradictory accounts of his motives of sojourn: a report that he is 'studying' hard – an intimation that he is much interested in a very clever foreign lady.

Appendix I
Henry James on 'Daisy Miller'

1. PREFACE TO THE NEW YORK EDITION (1909)

'Daisy Miller' was one of a number of shorter works (and first in the order of contents) gathered together in volume 18 of the New York Edition of *The Novels and Tales of Henry James*, published in 1909. The relevant part of James's Preface to that volume is as follows:

It was in Rome during the autumn of 1877; a friend then living there but settled now in a South less weighted with appeals and memories happened to mention – which she might perfectly not have done – some simple and uninformed American lady of the previous winter, whose young daughter, a child of nature and of freedom, accompanying her from hotel to hotel, had 'picked up' by the wayside, with the best conscience in the world, a good-looking Roman, of vague identity, astonished at his luck, yet (so far as might be, by the pair) all innocently, all serenely exhibited and introduced: this at least till the occurrence of some small social check, some interrupting incident, of no great gravity or dignity, and which I forget. I had never heard, save on this showing, of the amiable but not otherwise eminent ladies, who weren't in fact named, I think, and whose case had merely served to point a familiar moral; and it must have been just their want of salience that left a margin for the small pencil-mark inveterately signifying, in such connexions, 'Dramatize, dramatize!' The result of my recognizing a few months later the sense of my pencil-mark was the short chronicle of 'Daisy Miller', which I indited in London the following spring and then addressed, with no conditions attached, as I remember, to the editor of a magazine that had its seat of publication at Philadelphia and had lately appeared to appreciate my contributions. That gentleman however (an historian of some repute) promptly returned me my missive, and with an absence of comment that struck me at the time as rather grim – as, given the circumstances, requiring indeed some explanation: till a friend to whom I appealed for light, giving him the thing to read, declared it could only have passed with the Philadelphian critic for 'an outrage on American girlhood'. This was verily a light, and of bewildering intensity; though I was presently to read into the matter a further helpful inference. To the fault of being outrageous this little composition added that of being essentially and pre-eminently a *nouvelle*;[1] a signal example in fact of that type, foredoomed at the best, in more cases than not, to editorial disfavour. If accordingly I was afterwards to be cradled, almost blissfully, in the conception that 'Daisy' at least, among my productions, might approach 'success', such success for example, on her eventual appearance, as the state of being promptly pirated in Boston – a sweet tribute I hadn't yet received and was never again to know – the irony of things yet claimed its rights, I couldn't but long continue to feel, in the circumstance that quite a special reprobation had waited on the first appearance in the world of the ultimately most prosperous child of my invention. So doubly discredited, at all events, this bantling met indulgence, with no great delay, in the eyes of my admirable friend the late Leslie Stephen and was published in two numbers of *The Cornhill Magazine* (1878).

It qualified itself in that publication and afterwards as 'a Study'; for reasons which I confess I fail to recapture unless they may have taken account simply of a certain flatness in my poor little heroine's literal denomination. Flatness indeed, one must have felt, was the very sum of her story; so that perhaps after all the attached epithet was meant but as a deprecation, addressed to the reader, of any great critical hope of stirring scenes. It provided for mere concentration, and on an object scant and superficially vulgar – from which, however, a sufficiently brooding tenderness might eventually extract a shy incongruous charm. I suppress at all events here the appended qualification – in view of the simple truth, which ought from the first to have been apparent to me, that my little exhibition is made to no degree whatever in critical but, quite inordinately and extravagantly, in poetical terms. It comes back to me that I was at a certain hour long afterwards to have reflected, in this connexion, on the characteristic free play of the whirligig of time. It was in Italy again – in Venice and in the prized society of an interesting friend, now dead, with whom I happened to wait, on the Grand Canal, at the animated water-steps of one of the hotels. The considerable little terrace there was so disposed as to make a salient stage for certain demonstrations on the part of two young girls, children *they*, if ever, of nature and of freedom, whose use of those resources, in the general public eye, and under our own as we sat in the gondola, drew from the lips of a second companion, sociably afloat with us, the remark that there before us, with no sign absent, were a couple of attesting Daisy Millers. Then it was that, in my charming hostess's prompt protest, the whirligig, as I have called it, at once betrayed itself. 'How can you liken *those* creatures to a figure of which the only fault is touchingly to have transmuted so sorry a type and to have, by a poetic artifice, not only led our judgement of it astray, but made *any* judgement quite impossible?' With which this gentle lady and admirable critic turned on the author himself. 'You *know* you quite falsified, by the turn you gave it, the thing you had begun with having in mind, the thing you had had, to satiety, the chance of "observing": your pretty perversion of it, or your unprincipled mystification of our sense of it, does it really too much honour – in spite of which, none the less, as anything charming or touching always to that extent justifies itself, we after a fashion forgive and understand you. But why *waste* your romance? There are cases, too many, in which you've done it again; in which, provoked by a spirit of observation at first no doubt sufficiently sincere, and with the measured and felt truth fairly twitching your sleeve, you have yielded to your incurable prejudice in favour of grace – to whatever it is in you that makes so inordinately for form and prettiness and pathos; not to say sometimes for misplaced drolling. Is it that you've after all too much imagination? Those awful young women capering at the hotel-door, *they* are the real little Daisy Millers that were; whereas yours in the tale is such a one, more's the pity, as – for pitch of the ingenuous, for quality of the artless – couldn't possibly have been at all.' My answer to all which bristled of course with more professions than I can or need report here; the chief of them inevitably to the effect that my supposedly typical little figure was of course pure poetry, and had never been anything else; since this is what helpful imagination, in however slight a dose, ever directly makes for. As for the original grossness of readers, I dare say I added, that was another matter – but one which at any rate had then quite ceased to signify.

2. CORRESPONDENCE WITH
MRS ELIZA LYNN LINTON

Eliza Lynn Linton (1822–98) was an English novelist and journalist who was well known in her own day, and acquainted with several famous writers besides Henry James, including Charles Dickens, George Eliot, Walter Savage Landor, and Thomas Hardy. Her writings were much concerned with what was known at the time as the 'Woman Question'. In her early work she took a progressive position on women's rights, but in mid-life her views underwent a complete reversal. This may have had something to do with the failure of her marriage to a widower with seven children, from whom she separated after some six years, for she said later: 'I thought that the lives of women should be as free as those of men and that community of pursuits would bring about a fine fraternal condition of things, where all men would be like big brothers and no woman need fear. I have lived to see my mistake.'[2] These words were written to defend a series of highly controversial articles which she wrote anonymously for the *Saturday Review* in the late 1860s, attacking what she alleged to be a decline in the values and behaviour of women in contemporary society (i.e., middle- and upper-class society) and calling for a return to the traditional notion of woman's role as wife, mother, and housekeeper: 'It is the vague restlessness, the fierce extravagance, the neglect of home, the indolent fine-ladyism, the passionate love of pleasure which characterizes the modern woman, that saddens men and destroys in them that respect which their very pride prompts them to feel.'[3]

One of the articles, 'The Girl of the Period', acquired particular notoriety, and provoked a cartoon in *Punch*. The title became something of a catch-phrase, and was used as the title of a book in which all the articles were collected and published, still anonymously, in 1868. Mrs. Linton sensationally accused the contemporary girl of coveting and imitating the life-style of women of the *demi-monde* – by, for instance, wearing revealing clothes. 'She cannot be made to see that modesty of appearance and virtue in deed ought to be inseparable; and that no good girl can afford to appear bad, under pain of receiving the contempt awarded to the bad.'[4] Although no one accuses Daisy Miller of dressing immodestly, her behaviour incurs the condemnation of her Europeanized compatriots in exactly this way. It is not surprising, therefore, that Mrs. Linton read James's story with keen interest when it appeared some ten years after *The Girl of the Period*.

As it happened, Henry James reviewed Mrs Linton's book in its American edition, which was entitled *Modern Women, and What Is Said of Them*, in the *Nation*, 22 October 1868, and he did so scathingly. He speculated that the articles were the work of several hands, mostly male, and declared: 'They are all equally trivial, commonplace and vulgar.' He questioned the thesis that the Girl of the Period emulated the dress and behaviour of the *demi-monde*, and concluded: 'The whole indictment represented by this volume seems to us perfectly irrational. It is impossible to discuss and condemn the follies of "modern women" apart from those of modern men.' It was an impress-ive and devastating review, and like most of Henry James's contri-butions to the *Nation* at that time, unsigned. This was fortunate, for James made Mrs Linton's acquaintance in the late 1870s, when he had settled in London. He must have been aware that she was the author of *Modern Women/The Girl of the Period*, for this had been generally known for some time; but if she had seen his review in the *Nation*, she would not have known that he wrote it, and he would surely not have volunteered the information. They were on sufficiently friendly terms for her to address him as 'My Dear Mr. James' when she wrote to him, in the autumn of 1880, from Como, in Italy, where she was staying, asking him to arbitrate in 'a very warm dispute about your intention in *Daisy Miller*' between herself and 'the most valuable intellectual friend I ever had'. He replied courteously and at length.

This exchange of letters is exceptionally interesting for several reasons. Mrs Linton's letter illustrates how deeply James's story, and the issues it raised, engaged the attention of readers at the time. It also shows how the ambiguity of his narrative method, even at this rela-tively early stage of his development, created considerable room for interpretative disagreement. So scrupulously fair is Mrs Linton's account of her dispute with her friend, that it is impossible to infer her own position with any confidence. James's answer to her question is, for him, unusually full and explicit, as well as tactful. Because James destroyed most of the thousands of letters he received in his lifetime, one cannot often read both sides of his correspondence. Presumably Mrs Linton's letter survived because, for reasons she explains, she asked him to return it to her with his reply.

Mrs Linton's letter is reproduced here from George Somes Layard, *Mrs Lynn Linton, Her Life, Letters and Opinions* (London: Methuen, 1901), pp. 232–3, and Henry James's reply from Philip Horne, *Henry James: A Life in Letters* (London: Allen Lane, 1999), pp. 122–3. The date of Mrs. Linton's letter is unknown, but was probably in late September 1880.

Como.

My dear Mr. James, – As a very warm dispute about your intention in *Daisy Miller* was one among other causes why I have lost the most valuable intellectual friend I ever had, I do not think you will grudge me half a dozen words to tell me what you did really wish your readers to understand, so that I may set myself right or give my opponent reason. I will not tell you which side I took, as I want to be completely fair to him. Did you mean us to understand that Daisy went on in her mad way with Giovanelli just in defiance of public opinion, urged thereto by the opposition made and the talk she excited? or because she was simply too innocent, too heedless, and too little conscious of appearance to understand what people made such a fuss about; or indeed the whole bearing of the fuss altogether? Was she obstinate and defying, or superficial and careless?

In this difference of view lies the cause of a quarrel so serious, that, after dinner, an American, who sided with my opponent and against me, came to me in the drawing-room and said how sorry he was that any gentleman should have spoken to any lady with the 'unbridled insolence' with which this gentleman had spoken to me. So I leave you to judge of the bitterness of the dispute, when an almost perfect stranger, who had taken a view opposite to my own, could say this to me!

I know that you will answer me. And will you send back this letter? I will forward it and your reply to my former friend, for unless he saw what I had written, he would believe that I had given you an indication of my view and that out of personal kindness you had responded in a sense favourable to me.

I write to you from lovely Lake Como, but as my time here is uncertain, and when you receive this still more so, I give you the only permanent address that I have.

I hope that you are well and happy. I have read your *Confidence* and *The Madonna of the Future*, etc., since I saw you. My admiration of your work increases if that were possible. – Most sincerely yours,

E. Lynn Linton.

Reform Club
Oct. 6th

My dear Mrs. Lynton,

I will answer you as concisely as possible – & with great pleasure – premising that I feel very guilty at having excited such ire in celestial minds & painfully responsible at the present moment.

Poor little D.M. was (as I understand her) above all things *innocent*. It was not to make a scandal – or because she took pleasure in a scandal – that she 'went on' with Giovanelli. She never took the measure, really, of the Scandal she produced, & had no means of doing so: she was too ignorant, too irreflective, too little versed in the proportions of things. She intended infinitely less with G. than she appeared to intend – & he himself was quite at sea as to how far she was going. She was a flirt – a perfectly superficial and unmalicious one; and she was very fond, as she announced at the outset, of 'gentlemen's society'. In Giovanelli she got a gentleman who to her uncultivated perception was a very brilliant one – all to herself; and she enjoyed his society in the largest possible measure. When she found that this measure was thought too large by other people – especially by Winterbourne – she was wounded; she became conscious that she was accused of something of which her very comprehension was vague. This consciousness she endeavoured to throw off; she tried not to think of what people meant & easily succeeded in doing so; but to my perception, she never really tried to take her revenge upon public opinion – to outrage it & irritate it. In this sense I fear I must declare that she was not *defiant*, in the sense you mean. If I recollect rightly, the word 'defiant' is used in the tale – but it is not intended in that large sense; it is descriptive of the state of her poor little heart which felt that a fuss was being made about her and didn't wish to hear anything more about it. She only wished to be left alone – being, herself, quite unaggressive. The keynote of her *character* is her innocence – that of her *conduct* is of course that she had a little sentiment about Winterbourne that she believed to be quite unreciprocated – conscious as she was only of his protesting attitude. But even here I didn't mean to suggest that she was playing off Giovanelli against Winterbourne – for she was too innocent even for that. She didn't try to provoke & stimulate W. by flirting overtly with G. – she never believed that Winterbourne was provokable. She would have liked him to think well of her – but had an idea from the first that he cared only for higher game; so she smothered this feeling to the best of her ability (though at the end a glimpse of it is given) & tried to help herself to do so by a good deal of lively movement with Giovanelli. The whole idea of the story is the little tragedy of a light, thin, natural, unsuspecting creature being sacrificed, as it were, to a¹ social rumpus that went on quite over her head & to which she stood in no measurable relation. To deepen the effect I have made it go on over her mother's head as well. She never had a thought of scandalizing any body – the most she ever had was a regret for Winterbourne.

This is the only witchcraft I have used – & I must leave you to extract what satisfaction you can from it.⁵

Again, I must say, I feel 'real badly', as D.M. would have said, at having supplied the occasion for a breach of cordiality. May the breach be healed herewith! –

You are detestably enviable to be at Cadenabbia. I hope you are either coming back soon or staying in Italy for the whole winter – as I expect to go thither for a long stay after the New Year. Wherever you are, believe in the very good will of yours faithfully

H. James jr.

NOTES

1. *Nouvelle* (French) is a prose fiction shorter than a novel.
2. George Somes Layard, *Mrs. Lynn Linton, Her Life, Letters and Opinions* (London: Methuen, 1901), p. 140.
3. E. Lynn Linton, *The Girl of the Period and Other Social Essays* (London: Richard Bentley & Son, 1883), vol. 1, p. 67. (This was a reissue of the original work published anonymously in 1868.)
4. Ibid., p. 4.
5. Philip Horne notes that 'HJ is often drawn to Othello's insistence that he won Desdemona not by magic but by his narrative art: "this only is the witchcraft I have used" [I.3.168]'.

Appendix II
The Play of *Daisy Miller*

There were, not just two, but three versions of 'Daisy Miller' by Henry James. In the early months of 1882 he adapted it for the stage – his first attempt at a full-length play. He was living in Boston at the time, following the death of his mother. Leon Edel tells the story in his magisterial edition of *The Complete Plays of Henry James*. James submitted his play to Daniel Frohman, manager of the Madison Square Theatre in New York, possibly after encouragement by the owners of the theatre. Frohman described the play as 'beautifully written' but rejected it because it was 'too literary'. James evidently felt betrayed by this experience and wrote later in his journal that it inspired 'deep and unspeakable disgust'.[1] It was an ominous augury of his later unhappy efforts to write for the theatre, culminating in the disastrous first night of *Guy Domville* in January 1895, when he was booed by the gallery on the stage of the St James's Theatre in London.

Reading the play today, one cannot be surprised at Frohman's decision, and indeed the words of his rejection seem kind. No doubt James's original story was too slight in substance for American or English theatrical taste at this time, but in endeavouring to inject more narrative excitement and interest James produced a vulgar travesty of the original. In modern idiom: in trying to sex it up, he dumbed it down.

First of all he resolved the fruitful ambiguity about what has detained Winterbourne in Geneva by creating a character called Madame de Katkoff, a glamorous Russian widow older than Winterbourne, with whom he has had some kind of affair, which she is trying to break off for his own good. It is revealed that Eugenio, the Millers' courier, was in the employ of Mme de Katkoff's deceased husband, and that he possesses a compromising letter from her which he uses to blackmail her. There are three acts. The first, set in the hotel garden at Vevey, introduces Mrs Costello with two more new characters:

Alice Durant, a young relative, whom she is hoping to marry off to Winterbourne, and a young American called Charles Reverdy, who is escorting the two ladies and is himself in love with Alice. Winterbourne meets Daisy and is both attracted and puzzled by her, as in the story. Mrs Costello is annoyed by this threat to her matchmaking plans. The second and third acts are set in Rome, in the Pincio and the Millers' hotel suite, respectively. Eugenio has introduced the fortune-hunting Giovanelli to Daisy and expects a cut from the lucrative marriage settlement that will follow. He regards the appearance of Winterbourne as a threat to this plan and blackmails Mme de Katkoff into reasserting her claim on Winterbourne's attentions, creating misunderstanding between Daisy and Winterbourne. Daisy behaves indiscreetly with Giovanelli, culminating in the visit to the Colosseum (reported, not presented) where she contracts the fever. In the last act she recovers but the misunderstanding between her and Winterbourne continues until Mme de Katkoff reveals all to Winterbourne, who rushes off to rescue Daisy from a dangerous excursion into the Roman carnival with Giovanelli. Winterbourne declares his love for Daisy and all ends happily with the prospect of marriage for them and for Alice and Reverdy.

It is not just the contrived plotting and coarsened characterization that make Daisy Miller: A Comedy in Three Acts a dismayingly bad play. James completely failed to find a plausible solution to the problem of how to dramatize a story in which most of the action is internalized in the hero's thoughts, making use of clumsy 'asides' and long soliloquies to reveal the motivation of Winterbourne and Daisy. The only positive feature of the play is some fencing dialogue between Winterbourne and Mrs Costello, whose tart rejoinders faintly anticipate Wilde's Lady Bracknell. James, however, seems to have been unchastened by Frohman's rejection, or by the failure of his subsequent attempts to interest a London theatre in the play. He was sufficiently pleased with it to have it printed for private circulation, and then published, first in the Atlantic Monthly, and then as a book, in 1883. A reviewer in the New York Tribune dismissed it as 'a highly impossible comedy' and commented devastatingly: 'we cannot repress some surprise – and regret – that such an accomplished writer and acute critic should not have perceived the full extent of the failure which he has now put permanently on record'.

The play of Daisy Miller throws no light whatsoever on the story. But there is some evidence that Henry James reread it, or at least looked at it again, in preparing to revise the story for the New York Edition. The second of Winterbourne's given names in the New York

Edition, 'Frederick Forsyth', absent in the original text, was first conferred on him in the play. It is just possible that James could have remembered this nearly thirty years later, but there is another, more convincing indication that he reread the playtext at that time. In the Preface to the New York Edition he describes Daisy as 'a child of nature and of freedom'. This phrase does not occur in the 1879 text, but it occurs in the play – applied, interestingly enough, to Randolph by Charles Reverdy:

REVERDY: Well, he's a dauntless American infant; a child of nature and of freedom.[2]

It is impossible that this phrase should have lodged in James's memory ever since he first penned it. He must have been struck by it in rereading his play and decided that it fitted Daisy better than her brother.

NOTES

1. Leon Edel, ed., *The Complete Plays of Henry James* (London: Rupert Hart-Davis, 1949), pp. 117–19.
2. Ibid., p. 126.

Notes

CHAPTER I

1. *Vevey*: A resort town on the shore of Lake Geneva, near Montreux. James stayed there, and visited the Castle of Chillon, in 1873.
2. *Newport and Saratoga*: Newport, Rhode Island, was a very fashionable Atlantic coast resort; Saratoga Springs, in upstate New York, was a much-frequented spa-town.
3. *Trois Couronnes*: 'Three Crowns' (French).
4. *Ocean House . . . Congress Hall*: Large hotels in Newport and Saratoga, respectively.
5. *the Dent du Midi and . . . the Castle of Chillon*: The Dent du Midi is a high mountain in the Alps, with a jagged peak. The Castle of Chillon is a medieval castle on a small rocky island just off the shore of Lake Geneva, made famous by Byron's poem 'The Prisoner of Chillon' (1816).
6. *Geneva*: The city at the south-east end of the lake. Henry James had attended a school there in 1859–60 while his older brother William was attending the University.
7. *the little metropolis of Calvinism*: The French Protestant Jean Calvin (1509–64) fled from France to Geneva and made it the centre of a radical and influential school of Protestant theology.
8. *the Simplon*: A mountain pass between Switzerland and Italy.
9. *Schenectady*: A town in upstate New York of commercial and industrial importance.
10. *the cars*: Railroad cars (i.e., railway trains).
11. *inconduite*: Wild or loose behaviour (French).
12. *tournure*: Figure (French).

CHAPTER II

1. *rouleaux*: Coils (French).
2. *Homburg*: A German resort town near Frankfurt-am-Main.
3. *Tout bonnement*: Quite simply (French).
4. *comme il faut*: Correct in behaviour (French).
5. *table d'hôte*: The common table in the hotel's dining-room (French).
6. *oubliettes*: Secret dungeons under trap-doors, where a prisoner might be forgotten (French).
7. *the unhappy Bonnivard*: François de Bonnivard (c. 1493–1570), the hero of Byron's poem, was imprisoned at Chillon from 1530 to 1536.

CHAPTER III

1. *Cherbuliez's ... 'Paul Méré'*: This novel by the Swiss novelist Victor Cherbuliez (1829–99) was published in 1865 and enjoyed considerable popularity. The story, set in Germany, has a certain resemblance to that of 'Daisy Miller': the heroine gives offence by her spontaneous behaviour and dies of a broken heart after she is observed by the hero in a compromising situation and suspected of impropriety. James was familiar with the novel, and this was a sly way of acknowledging his debt to it.
2. *Via Gregoriana*: A 'good' address, near the Spanish Steps.
3. *the infant Hannibal*: The Carthaginian general of the second century BC, who famously invaded Italy over the Alps with a train of elephants, hated the Romans from childhood because his father had been defeated by them in battle.
4. *the Pincio*: Gardens laid out on a hill adjoining the park of the Villa Borghese (see note 6), with winding paths that are a popular strolling place. The view westwards over Rome from the terrace at the top is celebrated.
5. *amoroso*: Sweetheart.
6. *Villa Borghese*: The palace built for Cardinal Scipione Borghese in the seventeenth century and its surrounding gardens, later made into a museum and public park.

CHAPTER IV

1. *Elle s'affiche*: She makes a spectacle of herself (French).
2. *St. Peter's*: The great Basilica of the Vatican.
3. *barber's block*: A wooden head for the display of wigs.
4. *as they did in the Golden Age*: 'The Golden Age' is a term usually applied nostalgically to a time in the past when the life of a society was more virtuous or idyllic or distinguished than at present; but Mrs Costello seems to be invoking it disparagingly to refer to an age of thoughtless hedonism, perhaps by association with pastoral poetry.
5. *cavaliere avvocato*: Gentleman lawyer (Italian). The title 'Cavaliere' was often bestowed on minor officials.
6. *marchese*: Marquis (Italian).
7. *qui se passe ses fantaisies*: Who acts according to her whims, who does what she likes (French).
8. *Doria Palace*: A famous seventeenth-century palazzo which belonged to the Doria family before it became a museum.
9. *portrait of Innocent X by Velasquez*: It has been observed that by placing his heroine, whose innocence is genuine but in doubt, under the famous portrait of the Renaissance pope Innocent X (who was in life far from innocent) by the Spanish painter Diego Rodríguez de Silva y Velázquez (1599–1660), James was 'making a pictorial pun' (Adeline R. Tintner, *Henry James and the Lust of the Eyes* (Baton Rouge and London: Louisiana State University Press, 1993), p. 26).
10. *du meilleur monde*: Of the best society (French).
11. *the Palace of the Caesars*: One of the ruins on an extensive site of Roman antiquities known as the Palatine Hill.
12. *the Caelian Hill*: One of the seven hills of ancient Rome.
13. *the Arch of Constantine*: A triumphal arch built to celebrate a victory of the Emperor Constantine in AD 312.
14. *the Forum*: This was the social, political and religious centre of the ancient Roman Republic.
15. *the Colosseum*: the ancient Roman amphitheatre (alternative spelling, 'Coliseum'), used for various spectacles including chariot races, mock battles, gladiatorial contests, and the execution of Christians by exposing them to wild animals.
16. *Byron's famous lines, out of 'Manfred'*: The passage in Byron's dramatic poem (1817) begins:

I stood within the Coliseum's wall,
'Midst the chief relics of almighty Rome;
The trees which grew along the broken arches
Waved dark in the blue midnight, and the stars
Shone through the rents of ruin . . .

17. *perniciosa*: The 'pernicious' fever, malaria (Italian).

AVAILABLE FROM PENGUIN CLASSICS

PENGUIN
CLASSICS

P.O. 0005076971 20210811